BURGLE THE BARON

BURGLE THE BARON

by

John Creasey

as

Anthony Morton

WALKER AND COMPANY
NEW YORK

First published in the United States of America in 1974 by the Walker Publishing Company, Inc.

Published simultaneously in Canada by Fitzhenry & Whiteside, Limited, Toronto.

ISBN: 0-8027-5312-4

Library of Congress Catalog Card Number: 74-80974

Printed in the United States of America.

10 9 8 7 6 5 4 3 2 1

Contents

I

The Plot

TWO MEN SAT in a small, inexpensive car in Hart Row, a narrow street in Mayfair, London, a few doors away and across the road from one of the most famous shops in the world, which was known as Quinns. Quinns was famous first for its rare antiquity as a building in the heart of a great city, for it was over four hundred years old, each timber, each tile, each wooden beam as it was when it had first been built, for this house had been owned by men who loved it ever since it had first been occupied, and had been as well-cared for as a favourite mistress, a beloved wife or a doted-on child. True, there had been some changes, even running water and a bathroom were now upstairs, but nothing had been changed or wasted and a few beams which had been cut or sawn had been preserved, as relics from a tomb.

Quinns was also famous because it was an antique shop owned by John Mannering.

Yet 'antique' and 'shop' were not quite the right words. In the first place, rare paintings and *objets d'art*, old jewellery as well as jewelled pieces, changed hands in the narrow and often shadowy building itself, the lighting designed to create the greatest effect: to show small pieces of priceless furniture, or miniatures perhaps by Watteau, or an ikon from a Russian church long since destroyed, or even on a single ring or a jewelled scabbard. Or there might be a piece of porcelain designed and made by a master a thousand years ago, having a lustre which had to be subtly brought out, to make it glow, rather than have a light shining upon it harshly, so that the brightness hid both blemishes and beauty.

The two men in the car were father and son, who had more than blood in common. They were criminals.

True, they were clever enough never to have been caught and to the best of their knowledge never even suspected; but they lived off the proceeds of crime and lived very well; in fact, in comparative luxury.

It was a bright spring day. Window boxes at the first floor windows of some of the other shops, mostly describing themselves as *salons*, were filled with daffodils and late crocuses, a few had primroses or polyanthuses in a great variety of colours, which caught the sun. Yet it was cold. The driver's window of the car was open only a crack, and although the two men talked, not a word was heard by passers-by. There was the trim, middle-aged woman with her small poodle not quite small enough to be a 'toy' and the two elderly women who turned into the milliner's nearly opposite Quinns, the young couple who stood outside a window where Indian and Persian carpets were on dignified display, the film starlet and her eager long-haired manager turning into a photographer's who was becoming famous. All these, as well as men and women walking briskly to or from a huge new building of reinforced concrete which had two garage floors underneath. This building occupied a bombed-out site which had been empty for years and where Mannering and many of his clients as well as some of his staff had parked their cars.

Since the huge block had gone up there, parking had been much more difficult in the area, and cars were more often seen unlawfully parked or standing — as was the little red one now — in Hart Row. By some accident of architectural design the new building was not visible from Hart Row, which was completely unspoiled, with no place in it newer than a hundred years old.

A policeman turned the corner from Bond Street, and the man at the wheel, Jonathan, the son, saw him in the driving mirror.

'The Law's approaching,' he remarked laconically.

'They'll do no more than move us on,' said David, the father. 'Have you seen enough, do you think?'

'For the time being, yes. But are you sure . . .?' the son broke off.

'In that shop Mannering never keeps less than half a million pounds' worth of stock,' the father asserted. 'And in the strong room there is at least another million pounds' worth.'

After a pause, Jonathan Cleff conceded, 'I've never known you wrong.'

'I'm not wrong about this, either.'

'Good. The Law is about to descend,' announced Jonathan.

He pretended to start in surprise when there was a tap at his window, and he turned his head and saw a youthful face beneath a curiously foreshortened policeman's helmet at the window. He wound it down hastily, and said,

'Oh, Lord! Am I breaking the rules?'

'I'm afraid so, sir. Only dropping and picking up is allowed along here it's so narrow. You must have seen the double yellow line. Are you going to be long?'

'If my wife could make up her mind more quickly we would have been away by now,' said David Cleff. 'I quite expected her to be out.'

'They do take their time, sir, don't they?'

'Is there anywhere near where I can wait?'

'If you drive into the forecourt of Hart House, that's at the end of Hart Row, sir, you'll probably be all right for a while,' the policeman advised. 'So long as you're not here for more than another five minutes.' He smiled his apologetic smile and walked on with the slow gait acquired very early in a policeman's life, while Jonathan wound up the window until it was open only a crack, and placed a hand on the gear lever.

'No point in annoying him,' he remarked. 'But the piece about a wife won us five minutes!' He looked across at Quinns, was silent for a few moments before going on. 'One and a half-million pounds' worth. Problem one: how to get it? Problem two: what to do with it once we have it? Problem three: how to make sure no one knows who took it? Dad — may I be frank?'

'You'll have changed if you're not!'

'This is too big a job for us.'

'On our own it would be,' David Cleff said quietly.

'But we always work alone!' Jonathan sounded alarmed.

'We always have a buyer,' David pointed out. 'So we can never be entirely alone. This time we need an expert of a different kind as well as a very big buyer. I don't think selling the goods will cause us much trouble. In fact I think we could find the market in advance.'

'Dad,' said Jonathan. 'I hate to say it but I think you're wrong about this.'

'Do you?' asked David the father. 'Drive up to Hart House, will you?'

His son obeyed, and immediately they passed Quinns, where a grey-haired man with very regular features was placing a jewelled casket on to a velvet-covered plinth in the window. This man was ex-Detective Chief Superintendent Bristow, now the manager of Quinns. A younger man stood behind Bristow, visible only in vague outline. Neither father nor son appeared to glance towards Quinns but soon they turned out of Hart Row into the forecourt of the mammoth building.

Huge though this was, it did not seem out of place. There was a simplicity about the lines, about the puckered stonework and the countless windows which was strangely mellowing. The forecourt itself was large and a dozen or so cars stood neatly parked, each space meticulously marked with a name except a spot saying *Visitors Parking*, which was close to another sign reading *Garage*. As Jonathan turned towards the *Visitors Parking* his father said:

'Go the other way round.'

'Into the garage, you mean?'

'Past the garage entrance,' said the father.

'You *are* being very mysterious this morning.' Jonathan's voice had a slightly exasperated edge. 'What have you got up your sleeve?'

'I'll tell you in a moment. Drive slowly past and look for anything unusual.'

Jonathan did as he was told.

Anyone observing them would have known at a glance they were father and son. Full-face, this was not particularly obvious, but as they glanced towards the garage ramp their profiles, caught in the same light and at the same angle, might have been carved from the same model. High foreheads, sharp recesses at the eyes, long but not over-long noses, short upper lips, full lower lips, sculptured chins. Jonathan's hair was raven black and his father's iron grey; and Jonathan had a leaner look at the cheek and beneath the chin where his father had a hint of a jowl. Otherwise, they were startlingly alike.

Jonathan looked away.

'The bulge in the wall?'

'Yes,' David answered.

'Behind Quinns?'

'Yes. There is a double reinforcement of concrete there to protect Quinns's strong-room.'

Jonathan pulled the car up near the *Visitors Parking* sign, turned and looked at his father with unfeigned admiration, all exasperation gone.

'How did you find out?'

'I checked the plans.'

'Where?'

'At the Westminster City Hall,' answered the older man. 'A property is falling vacant in Hart Row, two doors away from Quinns, and I said I was interested in buying and wanted to know what restrictions there were in the conveyance and whether I could build in the small yard — I said I needed a warehouse for television and radios. So they let me see the plans to prove there was no chance of going an inch beyond the present wall. The young man in the surveyor's department pointed out where the construction engineers had been forced to make the garage ramp too narrow at one place because they couldn't disturb Quinns, which is a historic building and preserved under the Act, whatever it is. So I wanted to check on Mannering's application to have Quinns registered as a building that has to be kept in its present condition.'

Jonathan breathed, 'And you didn't say a word of this to me!'

'I never do talk about a project until I'm sure it's practicable,' his father reminded him drily. 'Mannering had to deposit plans, of course, and the section closest to the Hart House garage ramp isn't part of the old building, it's an underground addition or extension. What else could it be but Quinns's strong-room?' David glanced at his son and laughed suddenly and with obvious satisfaction. 'It's almost certain that we couldn't get into Quinns from Hart Row, but we can get into that strong-room at a week-end, Jon. The new building is an office block, there isn't even a penthouse. Most of the offices are closed from Friday evening until Monday morning, all of them are closed from one o'clock on Saturday. There are two nightwatchmen, both on duty on week-nights, only one on Saturday and Sunday. We would have to deal with them and get through the concrete.'

Jonathan barked, 'How?'

'We'll have a builder's lorry painted with the name of the contractors who built Hart House,' answered his father. 'And we'll hire a pneumatic drill. Have you ever handled a pneumatic drill?' he inquired.

'I can learn,' replied Jonathan.

'You're going to have to be a builder's labourer for a week or two,' David told him. 'You need to be an expert. Once we're through we'll bring everything two people can carry out of the strong-room and put it in the truck. There's no way of estimating how long it will take but with luck we shall be in and out by Saturday evening.'

Jonathan moistened his lips, was silent for a few moments, and then asked in a hoarse voice,

'What about the things in the shop?'

'If we can get into the shop easily, we'll take them. If we can't, we'll leave them.'

Jonathan gulped.

'And — and what about a buyer?'

'I think I know a buyer, as I told you,' answered David Cleff. 'But that's one of the things it's better for you not to know about yet.'

For a moment it looked as if Jonathan would argue, but he raised no protest and instead sat farther away from his father and looked at him with that unfeigned admiration, marvelling. David raised his hands palms upwards, and shrugged. They were still there when the young policeman appeared from an alley on the far side of the new building, a short cut to Piccadilly and to Park Lane. If he recognised them he showed no sign but walked at a much faster gait than when he had first passed them. And he did not appear even to glance at them.

Suddenly, Jonathan blurted out: '*When*, Dad?'

'Within the month, I should say.'

'Must we wait as long as that?'

'You have to learn how to use a pneumatic drill,' David reminded his son.

'And you have to find that buyer!'

There was something else which David Cleff had to do, but he did not dwell on it then although he had already mentioned it in passing. He had to 'take care' of the nightwatchmen, and in some ways this would be the most difficult as well as the most distasteful of it all. David did not wish to kill them. He had on occasions used violence but only to save himself never as a means of pulling off a coup. He did not yet see how he could handle the men without violence, and so far all he knew was that they existed; he did not know who they were nor where they lived.

Certainly it would be a month before everything was ready. That would be in early May, say early to middle May. He must find a way to make sure that Jonathan did not get too impatient, and probably the best way would be to find one or two smaller — much smaller — assignments to do. He knew his son extremely well. In another two or three years the boy might have to go off on his own, but until that day came they would continue to make a perfect team.

The Quinns job might even work a miracle, might even make it possible for them both to get out of 'the game' for ever.

He was not really a believer in miracles. He would probably be too restless, anyhow; having plenty of money and so being able to lead an idle life would not of itself appeal to him for long. He did not think it would appeal to Jonathan, either, but Jonathan hadn't yet met the girl he wanted to marry. Once he did, his attitudes might change radically. If he were wealthy from the Quinns haul then the chances of his leading a happy life were surely much the greater.

The one thing which did not seriously occur to David Cleff was that the Quinns affair might fail.

As they passed the narrow-fronted shop with the name in Elizabethan lettering on the dark fascia board, a man approached, tall, lean, quite outstandingly handsome even at a distance, startlingly so when at close quarters. He paused for a moment to look at the jewelled casket and then turned into Quinns briskly. He shot one glance at the little red car before disappearing.

'Dad!' exclaimed Jonathan, almost gasping.

'Yes,' David Cleff said. 'I know. That was John Mannering.'

2

John Mannering

John Mannering noticed the little red car as he recognised the similarity of the two men in it, on the perimeter of his vision. That was how he noticed most things, although he could pull many sharply into focus whenever he wanted to, provided they had registered firmly enough in the beginning. At that moment he also noticed the young couple coming out of the oriental carpet shop, recently the scene of some violent crimes, and the attractive girl in stockinged feet who was taking a hat off a stand in the milliner's window. He never ceased to marvel at the amount of money women would pay for the ephemeral value of a hat. He was not marvelling this morning, however, but was deeply preoccupied; even his glance at the Egyptian casket which Bristow had put in the window was cursory. Bristow was talking to a girl at the back of the shop. Two of the younger assistants at Quinns, virtually apprentices, were dusting stock; the sight of young men in immaculate neo-Edwardian dress, hair beautifully combed and brushed, using dusters like a parlour-maid was always incongruous. A third young man was standing by the side of a frail-looking youth in front of four miniatures: gems by an unknown Dutch artist.

The girl turned from Bristow, anxiety obvious in a pretty face.

'Oh, Mr. Mannering. I can't tell you how grateful I am that you've come.'

'I wish I could have got here earlier,' Mannering said, taking a ring of keys from his pocket and turning to an oak door on the right. 'Do come in.'

This end of the shop was divided by an aisle — which indeed ran from the front door — leading to a doorway, and, beyond, to the storerooms on the ground floor and a small flat above. This flat was now occupied by an old man who until recently had been the manager. Opposite the door which Mannering opened and which led to his office was a very long Welsh dresser, brought from a Hereford farmhouse and made about the sixteenth century. It was as beautifully carved at the back as at the front, and the back panel provided a kind of screen. Small packages were wrapped on the bench-like front and some small oddments of stationery and wrapping paper were kept there. The original maker of this had provided, in the carving of flowers and faces, a number of small holes and through these anyone behind the dresser could see into the main part of the shop. There was also a combination microphone and loudspeaker which caught the conversation of anyone outside the window and brought it, muted, to the back. If there were the slightest hint of alarm, this could be turned up so that everyone in the shop could hear.

There were few precautions which Mannering had not taken.

He was not thinking of precautions then, but of the girl. Bristow had called him at a sale where he had been bidding for some Georgian silver and several Stubbs paintings, saying very simply,

'Deirdre Ballantine is here, John, very distressed. She won't tell me what is worrying her, except that she has a message from her father.'

Deirdre was the daughter of Sir Lucas Ballantine, one of Mannering's oldest and most valued clients. They were social acquaintances, too, although not strictly speaking friends. Mannering knew the girl well enough to be quite sure that she would not raise an alarm without good cause. He closed the door on Bristow and pulled a chair up to a bow-shaped, Queen Anne period desk, before sitting behind the desk. For the first time he was able to see Deirdre in a good light — 'daylight' fluorescence — for there was no window in this room.

Over in the corner, fastened to the floor, was a large Regency armchair. It stood over the only entrance to the strongroom here.

He thought: she hasn't had much sleep. Her eyes were red and glassy, and she had put on make-up carelessly, which was not characteristic of the girl, who was in her early twenties, more blonde than brunette, with particularly nice blue eyes and rather a short nose which showed her nostrils. In some moods she had a sulky expression and her chin was inclined to slope into her neck. But especially when well made-up she was attractive and she could be deliberately seductive.

She leaned back and closed her eyes. He thought tears were forcing their way through the lids. This was a moment to sit and say nothing, but he wished he had asked Bristow for some coffee. He lifted the telephone which was connected with Bristow's desk — behind the Welsh dresser — and Bristow answered at once.

'Coffee, Bill, please.'

'Josh is getting some,' said Bristow.

'I should have known.' Mannering rang off, watching the girl for a moment and then turning to the letters on his desk. Bristow had put them there earlier but he, Mannering, had not had time to look through them. Two were from the United States, telling him of dealers who would be in London in the next few days; all were from dealers either offering goods they knew would interest him or asking him what he could offer over a range of *objets d'art*. He absorbed the details quickly and put each letter aside.

There was a tap at the door and an old, white-haired man with a gentle expression came in with a tray of coffee; a silver tray, china pot and cups and saucers, cream jug and sugar basin. There were some plain biscuits, too. The girl did not look at him and he did not speak, but just went out as Mannering said: 'Thank you, Josh.' Then he asked, 'Do you like cream in your coffee, Deirdre?'

She screwed up her eyes.

'I — I'm sorry. I didn't hear you.'

'Do you like cream in your coffee?' he repeated.

'Oh. Yes, please.' She opened her eyes, watched him pour out, and took the cup. Her fingers were unsteady even as she carried the cup to her lips.

He pushed the biscuits closer to her, then poured out coffee for himself. The only thing he felt quite sure about was that she had refused to talk to Bristow because she did not like what she had to say. He let some known facts slip through his mind. She was Ballantine's only daughter, in fact his only child. He had been widowed for ten years or more, and since she had left school she had lived at his London house with him, had attended many functions with him where a wife would usually have been at his side. Could this visit be concerned with her family affairs? He did not think there was any likelihood at all of that: he simply was not on close enough terms with the family.

Suddenly, she put down her cup.

'My father did not send me,' she stated. 'I came without his knowledge.'

He needed no more telling why she had refused to confide in Bristow, and he was more puzzled than ever, but the important thing was to keep her free from these near crying fits. So he said quietly,

'If I can help, of course, I will.'

She drew a deep breath before saying in a husky voice,

'Oh, you mean that now, I'm sure you do. But you can't help, not really help. I shouldn't have come. I — I just felt that I had to talk to someone, and I know that Daddy has a great respect for you. And — you are involved already, in a fashion.' She shrugged her shoulders, looking very pretty in a forlorn kind of way, and for the first time she smiled slightly. 'You didn't expect to hear that, did you?'

'No,' Mannering said, simply to humour her.

'You *are* involved.'

'How?'

'You have a lot of Daddy's collection in your strong-room, haven't you?' she asked, and before he could answer, almost before she had finished what she was saying, she sprang up from her chair and drew closer to him, standing over him with her hands clenched and her eyes aflame. 'But they're not simply his, a lot of them are mine. Morally if not legally. *Aren't they? You* know, *you* know the truth. A lot of them are family heirlooms and that means they're really mine as well as his. Isn't that true?' She actually shook a clenched fist in front of Mannering's face and peered very closely into his eyes, demanding not only an answer but the answer which she wanted.

'I only know that a great number are family possessions,' he replied equably.

'That means they're mine!' she cried

'And I know that I am keeping them in trust for your father.'

'You're as bad as he is!' she cried. 'You won't admit they're mine as much as his.'

He wanted to try to comfort her because she was in such distress, yet there was also a part of him which felt like putting her across his knee as one would a spoilt child. Looking up into her glaring eyes he saw how bloodshot they were, realised even more vividly how exhausted she was; the temptation to treat her harshly faded.

'Deirdre,' he asked quietly. 'What is troubling you?'

'You know what the trouble is!' she stormed.

'I haven't the faintest idea,' he assured her.

She drew back and words formed on her lips. He thought she was going to accuse him of lying, but the words did not come. She drew back and a furrow appeared between her eyes, ageing her, somehow persuading him that she was genuinely puzzled. Instead of waiting for her to comment, he asked,

'Why don't you tell me, Deirdre? If I can help, I promise you I will.'

'You — you really don't know what I'm talking about?' she marvelled.

'I really have no idea,' he assured her. 'But I'm getting more and more interested every moment. Will you have some more coffee?'

She hesitated, then held out her cup and picked up a biscuit, ate it in a gulp and took another; suddenly he realised that she was ravenous, and wished he had sent for sandwiches. She took up her cup again and spooned in sugar, then burst out,

'You mean that Daddy didn't tell you he was getting married again?'

Mannering exclaimed blankly, 'Good Lord, no!' On the instant he understood the basic reason for the trouble; fear that she would lose what she believed to be rightly hers to another woman, a step-mother who would inevitably cut across the close father-and-daughter relationship. The understanding came with such impact that he could not hide his astonishment, and Deirdre looked at him, blank-faced, perhaps fully satisfied for the first time that he had not even suspected the truth.

'No,' Mannering said at last, 'I hadn't been told and I've heard no rumours.'

She gulped down a biscuit before saying: 'Well, he is. And ever since they became serious he's — he's taken himself in hand, he's much fitter and has lost a lot of weight. He's become almost with-it, too! I feel such a bitch.'

'*You* do!' exclaimed Mannering.

'Yes.'

'Don't you like her?'

'Daddy loves her so much and I hate the sight of her!'

'Out of sheer prejudice?' asked Mannering, heavily.

She stood firmly in front of him and smiled for the first time since she had come into the room, a rather pleasant, ironical smile; not bitter, not resentful. There were some nice qualities in Deirdre Ballantine. She picked up another biscuit but before biting a piece off, she replied,

'I suppose so. She *has* put my nose out of joint.'

'Has she taken over from you?' asked Mannering.

'In a way,' answered the girl. 'In one way she has tried desperately hard not to — or at least I think she has and she's certainly done her best not to let me think she's taking over. In fact it's all a kind of sham. They are living together really although they keep up a pretence of having separate flats, and Daddy has been unbearably sweet, assuring me that it won't make the slightest difference to me. And *that*,' she added with sudden fire, 'is absolute nonsense! It can't fail to make all the difference in the world. And it *should*. Good God, if Daddy remarries he wants a wife not a stand-in for a daughter! Why don't they come out with it openly and admit that this will make a world of difference, that it would really be much better if I had a flat somewhere away from here. That's the obvious thing to do, isn't it?' she demanded fiercely.

'For a while, probably, yes.'

'I will say you are as honest about it as anyone I could hope for,' said Deirdre. 'That's partly why I came to you, you've a reputation for telling even unpleasant truths, I . . .' she broke off, then stood up again and began to walk about the office. The Regency chair suddenly attracted her: she sat back in it, able to swing her attractive legs. 'I really shouldn't have come and cried on your shoulder.' She added, 'It's unforgivable.'

'It's forgiven. In fact I'm very flattered.'

'You are very gallant, certainly.'

'I'm still extremely curious.'

'About why I came to you?' asked Deirdre, glancing upwards. Something on the wall attracted her attention but she went on without referring to it. She was much more composed in every way and her voice was pleasant, lacking the harshness. 'I heard them talking last night.'

'Oh?'

'About some of the family rings and jewellery.'

'Ah.'

'And he said she would look beautiful in them,' Deirdre went on with a catch in her voice.

She gulped, and now slid from the chair and stared at a portrait of Mannering which hung above his head. Lorna, his wife, had painted it at least ten years ago and had dressed him in the costume of a cavalier, with beard and wig and hat and *fal-de-rols*; yet it was uncannily like him. She did not speak for what seemed a long time, and it was Mannering who broke the silence by asking very quietly,

'And would she look beautiful in the jewellery?'

In a muffled voice, Deirdre said, 'She would look beautiful in anything.'

'But the jewellery would set her beauty off?'

'Yes. *Must* you rub it in?'

'I would like to be sure,' Mannering replied gently, and when at last Deirdre lowered her gaze from the cavalier she found he was looking at her intently, and she coloured. 'Deirdre, what do you really expect of me?'

'I don't know,' she responded helplessly. 'I simply couldn't think of anyone else to come to. I know you keep the jewels in your strong-room, I knew he couldn't get them out without you, and I felt desperate. I just had to come and see you, I suppose I thought you — you might at least reason with Daddy, talk to him, try to make him see that they *are* mine, that it's not right they should go to her.' Tears were back in her eyes now and her voice became husky. 'It really isn't right, they *are* family possessions.'

There was no way for Mannering to judge whether it was legally right or not, and certainly there was not the slightest justification for him to interfere. He believed that the girl knew that now, and realised she had come on a forlorn hope. What on earth had possessed her to come to him in the first place? Why not the family solicitor? Or a relative? Or a close friend?

'Deirdre,' he said. 'I simply don't know the answer, but I do know that I've had business with your father for nearly twenty years and I can't imagine a man I'd rather deal with. As for keeping some of his treasures here — yes I do. I keep things which belong to a great number of people in my strong-room, I doubt if more than a third of what I have there belongs to Quinns or me.' So that she could understand more clearly he went on, 'Some things are kept for a few days and nights, for clients in transit. Others are kept there to be sold on behalf of their owners who tell me they can't think of a safer place. Sometimes friends who prefer to use my strong-room to a bank or a safe deposit their treasures there. Your father . . .'

'Oh, I know, he's one of many,' Deirdre said. 'He's told me more than once that he thinks your strong-room is the one impregnable place in London. And of course you couldn't let me take them away, I wouldn't dream of asking, but — but could I possibly see them? *Could I?* I can't bear to think that the next time I see them they will be on her.'

3

Dilemma

IF HE ALLOWED HER to see the jewels, Mannering realised only too well, it might upset her very much; when she had first come she had been near hysteria, and it would not take a great deal to drive her back to that same mood. If he refused, he might make her bitter, even angry and resentful, but she would probably come to realise that he had little choice. She watched his expression with great intentness, hope blazing in her eyes, but slowly the hope faded and near despair took its place. Before he spoke she turned away, without speaking.

'Deirdre . . .' he began.

'It doesn't matter,' she said flatly. 'I shouldn't have asked.'

'I'll gladly call your father and if he agrees . . .'

'No!' she exclaimed. 'You mustn't do that.'

'Why not?' asked Mannering. 'He doesn't know how you feel, does he?'

'No, and I don't want him to!'

'The only hope you have of getting back to a good relationship with him is to confide in him now,' Mannering told her.

'It's just not possible. He — he isn't seeing anything straight, he can't be! If he really believes that his remarriage will make no difference to me, he must be blind. That's what they say, isn't it? That love is blind?'

Mannering looked at her very straightly, and held her gaze for so long without speaking that she began to colour slightly. Finally, he leaned back in his chair and said.

'Do you want to hear the truth or do you want to fool yourself?'

'I want to know the truth. I *am* facing the truth!'

'I don't know you very well, I don't know your father as a person so much as a businessman and a collector, and I don't know your future step-mother at all,' Mannering said. 'So I can't be prejudiced, can I?'

'I suppose not,' she conceded grudgingly. 'I . . .' she broke off.

'Deirdre,' Mannering said. 'I've an uneasy feeling that you're behaving like a spoiled child. That your father's impending marriage has thrown you off balance and you can't see anything clearly or in its right perspective. I don't know whether you're giving the woman a chance, and I don't even know whether it's possible for you to. I'm quite sure you're being unjust to your father. He might really believe there's no reason why your relationship shouldn't continue to be happy. When he says it won't change he probably doesn't mean the day-by-day living, he almost certainly means the basic love and affection and trust. At the very least you should find out what he does mean. And if he were to know how you feel about the family jewels it might help mutual understanding. That's why I think I should talk to him on the telephone — or at least tell him why you're here and say you want to talk to him about the situation.' When she didn't answer, simply stood with her hands raised in front of her bosom and her lips parted as if in astonishment at all he said, he ventured one more sentence, even though it was like talking to a woman who had been turned to stone. 'May I call him now? If you prefer it I'll just say you're here and would like to see him.'

He stopped; and the only sound was their breathing, his light and regular, hers beginning to labour as if the drawing of breath was a great physical effort. The silence went on for a long time, enough for him to ask himself whether he should have made any attempt to help, simply to soothe.

At last, she said, 'So I'm behaving like a spoilt child.'

He didn't respond.

Her breathing became more laboured and the colour faded from her cheeks which became ashen grey, leaving her eyes very bright. He was afraid he had done much more harm than good; he couldn't retract or it would sound hollow, but he should never have used that phrase. Suddenly, she swayed, and screwed up her eyes and half-turned away from him, and her pallor was so great that he was alarmed and sprang up. She seemed now to be groping for the big Regency chair but stumbled before reaching it, so he put an arm about her shoulders to steady her. Before he knew what was happening she was crying and he was supporting her, and he had to ease her round for his own as well as her comfort, so that she stood with her arms huddled against his chest crying, sobbing. He did not try to move again or to solace her, but simply let her cry. She cried for a long time.

His telephone bell rang; low-pitched but startling.

He made no attempt to answer it.

The call must have come through Bristow who would not have interrupted unless it were important. *Brr-brrr: brrr-brrr.* The girl stirred, and there was a break in her crying as well as less distress. *Brrr-k.* The ringing stopped. Mannering felt the girl relax and led her to the big chair which stood over the strong-room. Until this chair was moved, and it was electronically controlled, there was no way of getting below even for him. He eased her down into it. Her cheeks were shiny with tears but at least her colour was better. She said something he didn't catch but might have been 'I really am', as he moved to his desk, opening a drawer and taking out a box of paper handkerchiefs.

There was a tap at the door.

'Just a moment,' he called, and took the handkerchiefs to Deirdre then crossed to the door. This would be Bristow, and Deirdre would not thank him for allowing anyone else to see her like this. He opened the door and Bristow stood a yard away, his back to the Welsh dresser.

'Yes, Bill?'

'*Her father's on his way*,' whispered Bristow.

Mannering began, 'Her father ...' and then broke off. 'Good Lord!'

'I couldn't hold him off,' Bristow went on apologetically. 'He asked for you and then asked whether his daughter Deirdre was here and I obviously didn't satisfy him when I said no.'

'All right,' Mannering said, with a sense of relief. 'It may be just as well. Is Josh upstairs?'

'Yes.'

'I may send Deirdre up to him.'

'I'll warn him,' Bristow said. 'You haven't forgotten ...' he broke off.

'What?'

'You've a luncheon appointment with Hishinoto of Tokyo at the Savoy, at half past twelve.'

'I had forgotten,' Mannering admitted, glancing at his watch. 'And it's half past eleven now. All right, Bill, thanks.' He went back into the room where Deirdre was at least looking dry-eyed although her eyes and lips were puffy and a child would have known that she had been crying. She sat back in the Regency chair with its stripes of gold and green and azure blue and looked at him quite boldly, although the effect was spoiled by a sniff. Then she looked at the wall over his desk, and asked,

'Is that an ancestor of yours?'

'No,' Mannering said. 'It's a portrait of me which my

wife painted — the fancy dress amused her! Deirdre, I hate to say it but there is a kind of emergency.'

'I know, I know, I've been here far too long already,' she said, getting up at once. 'If I can spend five minutes in your powder room — or doesn't Quinns *have* a powder room?' There was a hint of mischief in her eyes and he had to give her full marks for a quick recovery.

'It's not an emergency for me but for you.'

'Me!' Her eyes even red-rimmed, had beauty.

'Your father is on his way here,' he told her.

'Daddy!'

'Yes — and no, I did *not* send for him!'

She began with the words 'But why . . .' and then broke off. She stood up, and looked at herself in a small mirror, and she did not ask a single useless question, just, 'How long will he be?'

'If he was at home when he telephoned, probably twenty minutes.'

'And he knows I'm here.'

'He seemed to think you might be.'

'Then it's no use running away, is it?' she said quietly. 'But I would like to tidy up before he arrives.'

'There's a bathroom upstairs and everything you need,' Mannering told her. 'An old friend of mine lives there, the man who brought in the coffee, and he'll be expecting you. I'll stall with your father for as long as you need.'

She drew in a deep breath, placed the mirror in her handbag and snapped the handbag too, looked at Mannering very straightly, and said in a completely controlled tone,

'As the issue's been forced I should tell him what you think best, Mr. Mannering. And I'm very grateful to you. I know that I needed some straight talk.' The hint of laughter appeared in her eyes again and she went on, 'Of course, Daddy may need some, too!'

Mannering was chuckling as he saw her to the door,

where Bristow took over and led the way upstairs. When Mannering turned back the office seemed very empty. He glanced up at the portrait as he moved towards the big chair and sat down. He needed time to think, so whatever was on the desk would have to wait until this afternoon. His problem in this matter was to assess Ballantine as a man. He might resent his, Mannering's, interference, and it could conceivably lead to the loss of a valued customer, but the first concern now had to be the girl. The more he saw of her, the more he liked her.

His telephone bell rang again. Could it be Ballantine already? He crossed to the desk and lifted the receiver as one of the young assistants said, 'I'll see if he's in, madam.' There was a pause and a click, before Mannering said drily, 'I'm in.'

'I wasn't sure whether you would want to talk to anyone just now, sir. Mrs. Culbertson is on the line and she *says* she is interested in the Felisa Emeralds.'

In one short sentence the assistant, very new to Quinns, had said a great deal. Mrs. Culbertson was a wealthy Australian widow who spent much time in London and who was a serious buyer of jewels for personal adornment; on the other hand far more of her inquiries were born out of a desire to see than actually to buy precious stones, and she could waste a great deal of time and be a considerable nuisance. But Mannering, to whom jewels were a passion which had at times been near mania, had a sneaking sympathy for the woman's weakness.

The Felisa Emeralds were kept in the strong-room except when needed for a special showing.

'I'll speak to her,' Mannering said. 'Hallo, Mrs. Culbertson... The Felisas?... I don't blame you being interested!... Yes of course we can get them out for you. This afternoon did you say?... At half-past three?... I shall look forward to seeing you.' He rang off, with mixed feelings, even a touch of ruefulness. She might actually buy and there was a part of him which hated to part with certain jewels. Nothing else affected him in the same way; simply precious stones which to him had always seemed alive.

He wrenched his thoughts off the emeralds to the Deirdre and her father situation. There were some who thought Ballantine very stiff-necked, far too much a man of the old school who still lived in a half-remembered Britain of the Empire he himself had never really known. Yet in politics he had often helped materially with problems of the newly emergent countries and much of his money was invested in Pakistan and India. He was a superb judge of precious stones, especially of diamonds and rubies, and a good judge on most *objets d'art* but uneven in his judgment of antiques. Mannering knew him most as a man of quick decisions and also a man of his word. He had known him for over twenty years. Lorna, Mannering's wife, had known Lady Ballantine much better than he, Mannering, had ever known Ballantine.

Lorna! Why not talk to Lorna!

Why hadn't he thought of that before?

He was actually at his desk, touching the telephone, when it rang and he felt it quiver beneath his fingers. He hesitated before lifting it, and as he said 'Yes' heard Bristow say,

'Ballantine's getting out of his car now, John.'

'Chauffeur-driven?'

'Yes.'

'Alone?'

'Yes.'

'I'll give you time to bring him to the back of the shop and come out to meet him,' Mannering said. 'Is the girl upstairs?'

'Yes.'

'Make sure she doesn't come down until I'm ready,' Mannering said. 'And get a message to Hishinoto that I may be half an hour late.' He heard a faint buzz which meant that the front door had opened, and rang off. He glanced up at the portrait again, then straightened the papers on his desk before opening the door.

He had one of the surprises of his life!

The Ballantine he knew was a man who looked his age — the early sixties; a man running to fat particularly at the jowl and paunch, one with an old-fashioned appearance in dark suits and rather wide trousers, the jacket hung straight to conceal the overweight. The man walking towards him a step ahead of Bristow, for there was barely room for two to walk side by side on that central aisle, was leaner, dressed in the neo-Edwardian fashion which rivalled Quinns's young assistants. He had a hardier look than Mannering could recall. His hair, almost white, was a little over-long but brushed back from ears and forehead. Here was a handsome man who seemed to be in his early fifties; broad forehead, hooked nose jutting from the lean cheeks, chin thrusting.

He was saying, 'I had no idea you were with Quinns, Mr. Bristow.'

'I've been here for several months,' Bristow told him.

'A reversal of the principle of setting a thief to catch a thief!' Ballantine's teeth seemed very white as he smiled; then he saw Mannering and his expression changed, the smile becoming sardonic, but at least in no way hostile. 'Ah. Good morning, Mr. Mannering. It is good of you to see me at short notice.' His hand-grip was very firm; his whole manner as well as his appearance had changed very much for the better. If this was the influence of his wife-to-be then in one way at least it was a very good influence indeed. He ushered Ballantine into the office, feeling sure that this man would know exactly what he was prepared to do and would not budge from it when he had made up his mind.

Mannering closed the door as Ballantine looked across at the Regency chair and asked:

'Does that still control the entrance to the strong-room?'

'Yes,' answered Mannering.

'Does Deirdre know that?'

'I doubt it. I certainly didn't tell her,' Mannering said.

'It is never very easy to be sure what Deirdre knows, she had a remarkably retentive memory for things she heard ten and even fifteen years ago,' Ballantine told him. Then his smile deepened, the lips arching, and he went on, 'Did she come to ask you to show her the Ballantine family jewels?' It was almost impossible even to guess what was passing through his mind as he went on, 'And if she came to plead for that, did you humour her?'

He stood with his back to the chair, facing Mannering, and they made a commanding pair, much the same height, much the same build, Mannering more conventionally handsome and with his dark hair only flecked with grey.

They might almost have been father and son.

4

Father and Son . . . Father and Daughter

SEVEN MILES AWAY, in a detached house in Cobbold Road, Wimbledon, not far from the Wimbledon Tennis Club, David Cleff and his son pored over some photographs of the garage at Hart House, photographs taken by a miniature camera at the Surveyor's office. It was a brick-built house, one of many erected between the two world wars. At one time it had been divided into two flats, one downstairs and one up, with separate entrances. Now, although they often ate together in the downstairs flat, that was David's; Jonathan lived upstairs, and whenever either of them wished to entertain, for a night or for a week or two, they had this completely separate accommodation. The front entrance could be used by both and the main staircase offered the easiest way of getting from one flat to the other. This domestic situation probably did a great deal to make their relationship so satisfactory. David was if anything much calmer about the project, but excitement was beginning to build up in his son, who broke off suddenly and made a rasping noise with his throat and lips : *Rrrrccck! Rrrrccck!*

'How do I sound as a pneumatic drill?' he demanded.

'About six years old,' his father answered.

'You won't say that when I break through into that strong-room !'

'No, I won't,' agreed David Cleff cheerfully. But looking at the excited face of his son, he wondered. Did one's children ever grow up? Was that even the right question? Did a parent ever see a son or daughter as an adult, as an independent human being in his or her own right? Or was it his son really had gaps in his development, areas within his mind and character where he was still a boy and would always be.

David had a sudden mental image of the boy's mother, his wife.

And even over a bridge of twenty years, it hurt.

* * *

In Mannering's office, the two men faced each other and Ballantine's questions still hovered in the air. They had been uttered in the form of a challenge and Ballantine's next actions would depend largely on how Mannering replied. He reminded himself that what mattered most was Deirdre. However, the father in this new projection of himself mattered almost as much : perhaps, more.

At last, Mannering said : 'She was desperately upset.'

'Distressed enough to be unreasonable, no doubt,' Ballantine remarked drily.

'Distressed enough to make me want to help.'

'Mr. Mannering,' asked Ballantine in a harder voice, and with his lips tightening, 'did you show my daughter those jewels which I placed here with you in trust?'

'No, I did not,' Mannering answered.

Ballantine was startled, 'But I had the impression ...' he broke off, and a smile appeared in his eyes and at his lips, reminding Mannering very much of Deirdre. 'No matter. Did she ask to see them?'

'Yes.'

'May I ask how you responded?'

'I asked her to let me telephone you, for your consent.'

'To show her the jewellery?'

'Yes.'

'Indeed,' said Ballantine, and he gave a little laugh. 'How very wise. I should have expected no less, of course. May I ask how she reacted to that?'

'Before I could find out, I was told you were on the way,' Mannering answered. 'I think I know what she would have answered, but thinking isn't knowing.'

'I have a great respect for your intelligent guesses,' Ballantine retorted.

'I'm not sure it's an area about which I should hazard one,' replied Mannering.

'It being so intensely a family matter?'

'Yes.'

'Mr. Mannering,' Ballantine said. 'Deirdre has been bottling up her distress for a long time—four or five months, at least. I was so preoccupied that I didn't realise this until the distress was frozen in her, and we could no longer talk to each other. By mischance, the only friends or relatives with whom she might have talked are out of the country or ill, and this drove her distress deeper in. I don't know for certain what happened last night but I think she overheard me talking with my fiancé, and this so upset her that she couldn't sleep. She came to see you because she knows the jewellery is here. You've made it obvious that she was in great distress—very upset, didn't you say?—and presumably she thawed, and in thawing really let herself go with you. If she did...' Ballantine hesitated in his first moment of uncertainty, and smiled in that wry manner again. 'May I ask if I am reasonably right, so far?'

'You're exactly right,' Mannering admitted.

'Thank you. Then you must know a great deal more about my family affairs than anyone else not intimately concerned, and I know of no one better qualified to make an intelligent guess about what Deirdre would have said on the matter of consulting me before letting her see the jewellery.'

Mannering laughed, 'I didn't quite see what you were getting at for a few moments!'

'I shall try not to be so loquacious again.'

'And I'll try to be brief,' Mannering promised. 'I think your daughter would have said yes, talk to you but *don't* talk to anyone else.' He raised his hands in a gesture of apology as he went on, 'Deirdre didn't really divulge very much. No names, for instance, and very few details: she simply outlined a new situation to which she hasn't yet been able to adjust.'

'She is very, very prejudiced,' Ballantine observed.

'One way or the other, and intentionally or not she has been very badly hurt,' Mannering rejoined.

'Yes,' Ballantine said heavily. 'I suppose she has, and I . . .' he broke off — spreading his arms. 'Let's say I have been deeply preoccupied. Is she still here?'

'Yes. She showed no sign of wanting to run away.'

'Deirdre wouldn't,' Ballantine declared, and it was almost a boast. He looked intently at Mannering, and went on; 'Do you resent having become involved?'

'I shall be sorry only if I can't help.'

'Will you be present when Deirdre and I meet?'

'If you think it's wise,' answered Mannering.

'I think it could be very helpful,' Ballantine declared. 'In a way . . .' he spread his hands again and added with a dour smile, 'I feel almost as if Deirdre and I have become strangers.'

Mannering made no comment but went to the telephone and when Bristow answered, told him to tell Deirdre that her father was here and would be happy to see her. Bristow rang off immediately. Ballantine glanced up at the portrait but made no comment. He stood by the chair, so still that to Mannering it was like an acknowledgment of his own nervousness. There was no sound at all, the office was virtually sound-proof, until there was a tap at the door.

'Come in!' Mannering called.

The door opened for Bristow to usher Deirdre in.

She had worked wonders with her make-up but nothing could hide the puffiness of her eyes or the redness of their rims, or the fact that they were glassy from lack of sleep. She came in briskly, and Mannering noticed she was tall for a woman, with a nice figure concealed rather than accentuated by a sheath dress of a beige-coloured tweed trimmed with dark brown. She had brushed her hair until it gleamed as it fell to her shoulders, and that made her appear to be no more than nineteen or twenty. She glanced at Mannering but stepped towards her father, looking at him as forthrightly as he looked at her.

'Hallo, Daddy.'

'Hallo, Long Legs,' he replied.

On the instant, Mannering knew that 'Long Legs' had some personal significance. It was an olive branch, carefully considered. And it checked Deirdre in her steady approach and for a moment Mannering thought she would fling her arms about her father. Instead, she pecked his cheek with her lips and backed away. As an olive branch the 'Long Legs' hadn't been seized, but Ballantine showed no sign of disappointment.

'So you would like to see the family jewellery?' he remarked.

'Yes, please.'

'Why just now?'

'I have a special feeling of attachment to them.'

'I see,' he said. 'Did you hear me talking to Anthea about them last night?'

'Yes, I did. And I'm sorry if I appear to have eavesdropped, but I didn't think you or Anthea would have been overjoyed if I'd declared my presence in the writing-room.' When her father didn't reply she went on defensively, 'Well, the door *was* open. You didn't check whether anyone was in the writing-room. And you did plunge into confidences very quickly, there wasn't time for me to call out without . . .'

'Without what?' Ballantine asked.

'Risking a confrontation.'

'Deirdre,' Ballantine asked. 'Why are you so desperately anxious to avoid a confrontation, as you call it, at all costs? I am not. In fact I would welcome one if it means what I hope it means — just an attempt to understand one another. I am practically sure Anthea would welcome one, too.'

'Practically,' Deirdre echoed; it was nearly a sneer.

'I can't be absolutely sure what anyone else is thinking,' Ballantine argued.

'No, Daddy, you certainly can't be sure what Anthea is thinking — only of what she is saying.'

'You know,' Ballantine replied, frowning but showing no sign at all of being ruffled, 'until a few months ago I would have sworn that I could at least anticipate your reactions to any situation accurately, but I was wrong. I could be wrong about Anthea, too, but I don't think I am. I think she can fill a part in my life which has been empty and often very lonely for a long time, without driving you out. If you are driven out, Long Legs, I think it will be by yourself.'

Obviously he had taken Deirdre off her balance, and she seemed confused for the first time since she had come in; and for the first time Mannering wished he were not here, for this issue was so essentially between father and daughter, and of such great delicacy. Before the girl responded, however, Ballantine's mood appeared to change and relax. He turned from his daughter to Mannering, and asked in a brisk voice,

'John — may we see the jewellery? We needn't keep you long. And of course any time Deirdre wants to see them you're quite at liberty to show her. Just make sure she doesn't take them away, that's all!' He turned back to

Deirdre and went on in the same brisk tone, 'You didn't hear what I'd been saying to Anthea earlier, of course, what you heard was a continuation of a conversation we'd started before dinner. It was that the jewellery was the family's — no individual's, no trust's, just the family's. There is no legal reason why I could not sell some, or give it to Anthea or even to you, but traditionally it belongs to the family.' His eyes suddenly brimmed over with a merriment which Mannering had never seen in him before; he warmed very much to this man. 'That doesn't mean I shall not squander all my own money on Anthea, of course! I'm very much in love with her, you know. You *must* know that.'

Deirdre said chokily, 'I — I do know.'

'I'm very glad. Now! May we go into your treasure house, Mr. Mannering?'

'If we can be out again in twenty minutes, gladly,' Mannering said.

'Twenty minutes enough, Long Legs?' asked Ballantine.

'I should think so,' answered Deirdre. 'And if it isn't then Mr. Mannering will always let me see them again, won't he?'

They all laughed, yet there remained some strain in the atmosphere; all was not yet well.

The strain began to ease a few minutes later.

Mannering, sitting at his desk and using a control system which the others could not see, released the armchair, and at a word from him Ballantine pushed it to one side. Almost at once part of the floor which looked to be of centuries' old boards darkened with age moved back slowly and revealed a steel under-floor. In turn this moved, revealing a set of cement-covered steps.

Mannering, who had locked the outer door, led the way down.

Devices hidden in the walls and the ceiling were operated only by using a hand-ray projector, and doors — four in all — slid silently open, since the strong-room at this section was divided into four sections. In each there were safes built into the wall, each one under separate electronic control, and on the shelves and in small alcoves and recesses were jewels and *objets d'art* of such beauty that the first glimpse of them made Deirdre catch her breath and made even Ballantine pause. There were jewelled swords and crowns and coronets, caskets and breastplates; there were rare pieces of china and porcelain, wrought gold and wrought silver. There were figurines in solid gold and silver. There were miniatures of breathtaking beauty, sculptures, plaques, tapestries — it was like a museum as crowded as a Pharaoh's tomb or as the Vatican's treasure house.

Vases and goblets, daggers and rings, watches and clocks, these and countless other *objets* stood beneath lighting which was skilfully thrown so as to reveal in each not only its surface but its latent beauty.

All of these were Mannering's stock-in-trade — and all belonged to Quinns.

In the safes were the treasures which he held for others; in a tall safe, only the door of which showed at one side of the second room, were the Ballantine jewels. Few knew it, but this was the common wall with the garage, over ten feet thick. Mannering needed both a key and an electronic device to open this, and the others watched closely as the heavy door swung open. He drew out two trays, giving one to Deirdre and the other to Ballantine, closed but did not lock the door and went to another safe in this same section.

Neither took any notice of him.

He opened the second safe and drew out three flat cases which contained the Felisa Emeralds, and relocked the safe. When he turned round, Ballantine was placing a necklace of diamonds and rubies about Deirdre's throat, and she was handling some smaller pieces: pins and brooches. On a small table stood a tiara, a bracelet and some drop-earrings.

Mannering felt his own heart beating faster.

Some jewels *did* have life : others came to life on the body of a beautiful woman. These jewels, set by a master in Bombay two centuries ago, had both kinds of life and they seemed to pour fire into Deirdre's eyes. Her father fastened the clasp, and placed his hands on her shoulders and turned her round. He was set on indulging her, obviously desperately anxious to reassure her.

Suddenly, she sneezed, and the anticlimax was so great that he felt a drooping of his spirit. She opened her handbag to take out a handkerchief. She raised this quickly to her nose, while her father picked up the tiara as if he had forgotten there was some pressure of time.

Deirdre shook out her handkerchief.

At first Mannering did not even begin to understand and the truth flashed on him when it was too late. A little phial of pepper struck him on the face, others struck Ballantine, on the instant Mannering's eyes stung and he began to sneeze and all he could see was a great blur of movement. Ballantine was staggering about and the girl sweeping the jewels into her handbag.

Now he needed no telling why it was so large.

5

Woman of Spirit

DEIRDRE BALLANTINE HELD her breath and screwed up her eyes which were already stinging with pepper. She saw her father and Mannering staggering from the corner of her eyes, as she pushed the last of the jewels, a brooch, into her handbag. She thrust some paper handkerchiefs and a primrose-yellow scarf on top of this and closed the bag, a little of the scarf caught and showing. Her father was leaning helplessly against the wall, his whole body shaking with the sneezes, but Mannering was on his feet and groping towards her. She sprang towards him and pushed with all her strength against his right shoulder, and he toppled backwards.

She turned and scurried into the next chamber. The stairs seemed to gape in front of her and she went up them on her soles, making no sound. The office was exactly as it had been, the door closed. She glanced up at the portrait of Mannering dressed as a cavalier, blew it a kiss, and reached the door. The key, a big, heavy one of iron, was turned in the lock, and she touched it before looking at a much more complicated lock a little higher up. As far as she could judge that one was already unfastened. She turned the iron key, expecting it to cause difficulty but it was very easy, had obviously been recently oiled. She pulled cautiously at the door which was heavy but moved easily, and heard a man speaking nearby. She raised her own voice and said very clearly,

'It's no use — no use at all.'

She pulled the door open wider and stepped outside, then closed the door firmly behind her. The man who had admitted her to the shop — named Bristow, she believed — was at a telephone which stood on the big counter at a screen or dresser. She put a hand to her eyes, as if to hide tears, and walked hurriedly to the front of the shop. Other people were about, three couples and a few solitary individuals, and she realised that all three elegant young men involved glanced at her; one, near the door, said clearly,

'Excuse me, sir.'

He left the side of a man who was examining an inlaid lap desk of ivory and rosewood, to open the door for Deirdre. She was dabbing still at her nose and just managed to mutter, 'Thank you.' The young man said, 'Good afternoon,' closed the door and went back to the customer he had been attending. In a few moments a buzz of conversation hovered about the shop but there was no noise until a chiming clock without a face, *circa* 1640, struck the half hour in tones like a subdued Big Ben.

That was half-past twelve.

Bristow put down the receiver after talking to the headwaiter at the Savoy Dining Room, giving a message to Hishinoto who would undoubtedly be punctual. He frowned. Even to be half an hour late Mannering would have to leave very soon, traffic was impossibly thick. He kept glancing at the door, expecting to see it open again, and puzzled because neither Mannering nor the girl's father had followed her out. Even if father and daughter had quarrelled, Mannering would normally have escorted her to the street door as a simple courtesy.

'I'm going to see what's keeping him,' he said *sotto voce*, and strode towards the office door. It seemed a long time since the girl had left but in fact it could not have been more than two or three minutes.

The first thing he saw was the open entrance to the strong-room.

The second was Mannering emerging from it, tears streaming down his face and suddenly taken by a fit of sneezing. Bristow was so appalled that he stood gaping. Then he rushed to the door, pulled it wide, called, 'Mr. Quartermain!' and swung back to Mannering, reaching the opening in the floor as Mannering tried to climb up on all fours. The door opened again and one of the exquisites called,

'Can I help . . .' and then broke off, as if thunderstruck.

'Try to find out where Miss Ballantine went,' ordered Bristow, urgently. 'She may be trying to get a taxi. Hurry! And close the door.' He went forward and took Mannering's arm without saying a word. Beyond, on the floor of the strong-room, Ballantine seemed to be in a far worse condition than Mannering himself. Mannering was trying to speak but his voice was a croak and the words were not distinguishable. Bristow led him to a corner behind his desk where there was a tiny cloakroom and ran some lukewarm water into the handbasin, then went to the office door and turned the key in it, next hurried down the steps to Ballantine, whose expression was quite piteous. By the time Bristow had helped him up the steps, Mannering was back in the office, dabbing his face dry on a dark blue linen towel.

'Did you see Deirdre?' His voice was hoarse but the words were quite distinguishable now.

'God damn me, I let her go,' breathed Bristow.

'Have you raised any alarm?'

'No. I sent Quartermain to look for her, but . . .'

'Good,' Mannering interrupted. 'I don't want any alarm raised until I'm sure what's missing. She probably took only the Ballantine jewellery, and I doubt if Sir Lucas would want to make a charge. Go and help him while I check, will you?'

'Yes, of course,' Bristow replied gruffly. 'The little devil! She fooled me completely.'

'You weren't the only one she fooled,' Mannering said ruefully. 'She a young woman of spirit if nothing else!'

'Spirit,' growled Bristow.

'Did you send a message to Hishinoto that I'd be late?' Mannering asked.

'Yes — I said probably half an hour,' replied Bristow, and went to Ballantine's assistance.

Within ten minutes Ballantine was able to see and to speak clearly. Mannering was almost himself again and Alec Quartermain had come back to report that there was no sign of Deirdre. The people in the shop did not appear to realise anything was amiss; the middle-aged man bought the lap desk for a hundred pounds, and Ballantine sat in the Regency chair which was now back in its protective position, with a sherry in his right hand. Looking over the glass, he asked Mannering,

'Are you quite sure that only the Ballantine jewellery has gone?'

'There's no doubt at all,' Mannering assured him.

'Then I most certainly don't want to prefer a charge at this stage,' the older man said, and although Mannering noticed the 'at this stage' with some surprise, he accepted the situation.

'Must you?' Ballantine added.

'Prefer a charge — no,' Mannering said.

'I am grateful,' Ballantine said, and after a few moments went on in a voice which Mannering could only just hear. 'She surely can't keep them for long.' He looked speculatively at Mannering as if wondering whether he agreed, but Mannering made no comment. It was Bristow who returned to the office at ten minutes to one and said,

'You're going to be very late at the Savoy, Mr. Mannering.'

'Yes, I *must* go,' Mannering said, and turned to Ballantine with a hand outstretched. 'I couldn't be more sorry. I'll be glad to help in every way I can, but there's a man at the Savoy who flew in from Tokyo this morning and is flying back again tomorrow, and I must see him.'

'John,' said Ballantine, using his Christian name for the second time as he shook hands, 'I can't tell you how desperately sorry I am. I can tell you that I shall want to find Deirdre very soon, but without having the police involved. Will you help to find her?'

'Yes,' Mannering said.

'Thank you.' Ballantine paused before adding very grimly, 'I don't know what devil has got into her. I don't know what to make of the situation. I don't want scandal but there are limits to family and parental indulgence. If you should find her or she should talk to you on the telephone, tell her I said so, will you?'

Mannering hesitated, Bristow fidgeted, and at last Mannering said, 'May we talk about that later? Bill! If you could work a miracle and get a taxi . . .'

'A private hire car has been waiting in the forecourt of Hart House for half an hour,' Bristow told him, picking up the telephone. 'By the time you're in Hart Row, it will be on the move.'

'Bill,' Mannering said fervently, 'I don't know what I would do without you.'

He waited only for a few moments outside the shop, settled back in the big car, saw Bristow standing with Ballantine just inside the window, leaned back and closed his eyes. They stung badly. He felt a strip of pain across the front of his head and the bridge of his nose and a stinging sensation at his nostrils and lips; it would be hours before he felt fully himself. In spite of that he found himself smiling faintly; Deirdre Ballantine had come fully prepared!

Why did she hate this Anthea so?

Careful, Mannering warned, or you'll get yourself even further involved. He leaned back and closed his eyes, and after a while began to concentrate on Hishinoto. He did not know what the Japanese dealer wanted; he did know that whatever it was he would be in deadly earnest. He came from Kyoto, although much of his business was in Tokyo, and Kyoto in a way was still a backwater in Japan, an imperial and religious city with palaces and temples untouched by the ravenous greed of industry. It was ten past one when the car pulled up into the courtyard of the Savoy.

'Don't wait,' Mannering said to the driver.

'Mr. Bristow asked me to remind you that Mrs. Culbertson is coming at three-thirty,' the driver said.

'Have him telephone her and try to change it to four.' Mannering turned amid a subdued chorus of: 'Mr. Mannering,' and, 'Good morning, Mr. Mannering,' and, 'Good to see you again, sir,' from porters who all looked like giants, and hurried to the dining-room. There, at a small table near the river, was the Japanese, slim, grey-haired, with a very lined face which was reminiscent of beautifully-engraved porcelain. He stood up as Mannering approached, and bowed before shaking hands.

'I couldn't be more sorry . . .' Mannering began.

'Mr. Mannering, I have known you so long that I have no doubt only an important emergency would make you late. I can only hope the emergency has been a pleasant one.' They sat down, both facing the river, and the Japanese went on, 'I came only to see you, so I was not delayed.'

'You are very kind,' Mannering murmured.

'Now, please, you will have a drink and, please, give me the great pleasure of letting me be your host.' Hishinoto's

English had a slight American accent, but in words and phrasing was impeccable. He would not discuss business until after the meal, and Mannering ordered eggs benedict, which would be gentle on his sore mouth, and a sole cooked in champagne with some new potatoes from the South of France. With a mild Moselle, the meal was perfect and the after-effects of the pepper were nearly gone.

'Now, I come to the reason why I have asked you to see me,' said Hishinoto. The blandness which had smoothed out the wrinkles while they had been eating and talking generally faded, he looked very, very old, and the crow's-feet at the corners of his eyes might have been carved from stone, his whole face was almost the face of a graven image. 'Mr. Mannering, a temple to Jimmu Tenno in the island of Kyusha has been damaged by fire, and in putting the fire out and repairing the damage the priests discovered a hoard of precious stones, of jewelled swords and of priestly and religious relics. These have not been seen by man for at least two hundred years.'

Mannering felt his heart beginning to beat fast.

'It is likely that they will be acquired by the Japanese government for preservation in one of our State Museums,' went on Hishinoto, 'and only remotely possible that they will be sold to a private collector. There is however a third possibility which I favour, in fact which I had the honour to suggest and which is being considered: it is that the treasure be divided among the great museums of the world. Here, in London, the British Museum, in Washington, the National Museum, in Paris the Louvre, in Copenhagen the Prinsens Palais. I am sure I need not name the others. There is a great shortage . . .' he spread his hands and smiled gravely into Mannering's face — 'there is a better word.'

'Dearth,' hazarded Mannering.

'Ah! That is the one! There is a great dearth of Japanese regalia and religious treasures in world museums and I believe these antiquities would help us to be a little better known, a little better understood. *You* understand?'

'Perfectly,' Mannering assured him.

'I was confident that you would. Now to my point, Mr. Mannering. You will also understand that I would be grateful for help from you. There are few men if any who could assess the potential value of this collection and compare it with other, similar ones of other nations. In Japan, of course, we would be influenced by the religious and the historic factors, involved, but museums do not deal very much in sentiment. Whereas an opinion from you, so highly regarded in all countries, would, I am sure, be accepted. It is not, you see, intended to auction these treasures so that they achieve their own value: only that a reasonable price be asked from the museums, with which money we could buy treasures we would dearly love to have. If you regard the collection to be beyond price, and we cannot offer it at a price within reach of the museums...' —Hishinoto gave a delicate shrug of his shoulders—'then I must accept defeat and the treasures must stay in Japan. Not, perhaps, a very big defeat, but...' the Japanese broke off.

Mannering said slowly, 'So you would like me to come to Kyoto, or wherever the collection is, to value it.'

'No,' said Hishinoto, quietly. 'I would prefer to bring the collection to you.'

Mannering looked astonished, but before he could comment the Japanese leaned forward and spoke with great earnestness. He was lost in his subject, and a liking which Mannering had felt for him over many years was greatly strengthened. The light from the river shone on the bald front of his head, and accentuated the lines at his eyes and on his face; he looked more than ever like a beautifully made figure in porcelain.

'To study these treasures, Mr. Mannering, you will need not a day or two, or even a week, but several weeks. I know you well, and you will not attempt to form a quick judgment on things which are so rare. And you have the finest and most secure strong-rooms of any dealer and valuer I know. You could put the Jimmu Tenno Treasure as we now call this find in your strong-room and study it at leisure.' When Mannering did not answer immediately, Hishinoto went on with even greater earnestness: 'If these were to go to a museum for the time being, or to a bank of commercial vaults, it would be extremely difficult for you to have access, and it would be much more difficult to keep the matter secret. If you were to agree to take them, however, I could bring them myself with one or two of my assistants. We would charter an aeroplane or, perhaps, bring them on an ordinary commercial flight and go to Quinns straight from the airport. This would then appear simply a matter of business between two dealers. Can you not see the advantages?'

'If secrecy is essential,' Mannering conceded.

'It is a condition laid down by my government,' Hishinoto told him simply. 'If the Jimmu Tenno Treasure is to leave the country it must be secretly. The religious and historic associations are too great to permit otherwise.' Hishinoto leaned forward even further and allowed himself a rare gesture: he rested his hand for a moment on Mannering's arm. 'Unless there is some very powerful reason why you should not do this, please agree, Mr. Mannering. It is of superlative importance.'

Mannering said, quietly, 'I think you put too high a value on my judgment, but if it seems right — yes, I would like to.' And as a light glowed in the other man's eyes a glow appeared in his, and Mannering said with much more warmth: 'I can't really wait to see them. When do you want me to start?'

'I could have them here in two weeks' time,' said Hishinoto. 'And I would expect you to take at least a month and possibly much longer. Mr. Mannering, I cannot tell you how much pleasure you have given me and how grateful I am.'

To Mannering, the almost unbelievable thing was that the Japanese obviously meant it.

* * *

'Dad,' Jonathan Cleff said to his father, in the middle of that afternoon.

'What is it now?' asked David.

'Do you really think we must wait a month before breaking into Mannering's place?'

'At least a month,' his father answered, 'and it largely depends on how soon you learn to become an expert with a pneumatic drill. Instead of dreaming about breaking in tonight, why don't you start looking for a job?'

Jonathan stared; and then they both burst into laughter which had an edge of excitement to it.

When his father had gone down to his flat, Jonathan looked out at the garden, reflecting that this should be kept better. Across Cobbold Street was an immaculate one, maintained by an elderly Negro who never seemed to hurry but got a surprising amount done.

Should he go out for a spin? he asked himself, without coming to a decision. The little red car was parked in front of the wooden garage, at the side of the house, he either had to put it away *or* take it out.

He simply could not make up his mind.

6

Threat

MANNERING WAS BACK at Quinns.

Mrs. Culbertson had come and gone, and hummed and hah'd, and said she would think about the Felisa Emeralds. Just after she had left Bristow, who had watched her enter and leave Mannering's office, asked Mannering dubiously,

'Is she really wealthy?'

'Mrs. Culbertson?' asked Mannering.

'Yes.'

'She could buy me out and not disturb her bank balance more than a trifle,' Mannering declared. 'Don't be fooled by her floppy hat and her flowered print dress. But she hates spending the money. If she ever buys the Felisas it will be after she's seen them half a dozen times and tried to get the price down by at least twenty-five per cent.'

'I can't pretend that I like her,' Bristow remarked.

Mannering leaned back in his chair and said drily, 'I think I like Deirdre Ballantine very much.'

'Little bitch,' said Bristow, but without much feeling.

He went out with some letters on which Mannering had made notes for his guidance. After a lifetime at New Scotland Yard Bristow had come to manage Quinns only a few months ago and there was a great deal he did not yet know. But Josh Larraby, the retired manager who lived upstairs was ever-ready with help, while Bristow had been the Yard's specialist on *objets d'art* and precious stones. The Bristow whom Mannering was now getting to know could be much more laconic and colloquial than the Bristow of the Yard.

As the door closed, the telephone bell rang.

Mannering picked up the receiver, for the call could be answered from here or from Bristow's desk. Thought of Mrs. Culbertson and of Deirdre Ballantine had vanished, he was preoccupied entirely with Hishinoto and the Jimmu Tenno Treasure. No wonder a woman like Edith Culbertson could drool over jewels she had already seen: he was already excited about the Kyoto discovery.

'John Mannering,' he announced into the telephone.

'Mr. Mannering,' said Deirdre. 'I owe you an apology.'

Her voice was quite composed and she sounded as if she were in the next room. He was hauled out of the past of a remote Japanese island to the harsh present of what had happened here this morning, and how best to deal with this girl. Only she wasn't now simply a 'girl' who was torn by an emotional storm: she was a calculating young woman who had pulled off a very bold coup. These thoughts flashed very quickly through his mind and there was only a brief pause before he observed,

'That is one of the understatements of the year.'

'Really?' Her voice rose. 'What do you mean?'

'You owe me the Ballantine jewellery. When will you bring it back?'

'Ah!' breathed Deirdre. 'I hoped we would talk the same language, Mr. Mannering. I will bring them back the moment my father breaks off his engagement to Anthea Ross. As soon as the engagement is broken, I promise you. But if he marries her I shall throw the jewels into the sea, I would rather they were never seen again than that she should wear them.'

After a moment's pause, Mannering said, 'Deirdre, will you please . . .'

'Please make him understand that I mean it,' she said in a voice which left him in little doubt. 'Don't make any mistake, Mr. Mannering, I mean what I say.'

'Deirdre, if you . . .'

The line went dead, with his own words ringing in his ears and about the mouthpiece; words which had been meant to begin what would have been an empty threat. Her threat wasn't idle, though, but a long, long way from it.

How she hated Anthea Ross!

He replaced the receiver very slowly, felt an immediate temptation to call Ballantine and then decided that there was no hurry; a few hours would make no difference to the general situation, but it would give him time to think. It was no use thinking about avoiding involvement, he could not be much more deeply involved now. Ballantine did not want this reported to the police but the insurance company should be told and they would tell the Yard at once. He needed Ballantine's signed instructions very soon. He pulled a few letters which one of the young neo-Edwardians had typed in excellent spacing, wrote in the courtesies, signed and sealed them, then took them out. No one but the staff was in the shop. Young Quartermain, broader, shorter and with darker hair than the others, came up for the letters. Bristow, dictating into a small machine, broke off as Mannering sat on the edge of the dresser beside him.

'Bill,' he said. 'We need to find where Deirdre Ballantine is.'

'Not home?' Bristow asked mechanically.

'That's the last place she'll go.'

'I suppose so,' conceded Bristow, pushing his chair back but keeping his seat in an oak chair which was at least three hundred years old. 'You know she ought to be charged, don't you?'

'Once a policeman, always a policeman!'

'John, she could sell . . .'

'She won't sell them and there isn't going to be a charge yet, Bill. But I want Ballantine's instructions in writing — and I'd like to know where Deirdre is.'

Bristow flashed a smile. 'So that you can go and see her and tell her to be a good girl in the future?'

'Something like that.'

'I'll do what I can,' Bristow promised. 'But you won't trust that young woman an inch too far, John, will you?'

'No further than she can throw pepper,' Mannering assured him.

Bristow was already speaking into the telephone when Mannering went into the shop to have a word with each of the staff, a habit he had acquired years ago. Not only did it keep him in touch with the kind of inquiries which were being made and the interest shown but it made the younger men feel that he was taking a personal interest in them. As, indeed, he was. Some were the sons of wealthy men who would one day set them up in business, and others were the sons of established antique and *objet d'art* dealers. Most of the young men who passed through Quinns would eventually take jobs with other dealers in London or, for that matter, anywhere in the world. A year in the service of John Mannering at Quinns was open sesame to virtually any house of repute on any continent. Apart from this, Mannering enjoyed talking about the pieces being offered, answering questions, giving advice. None of these knew what had happened at Quinns that day, but each knew it had been something out of the ordinary.

To each of the four, Mannering said, 'If by chance Miss Ballantine gets in touch with you, let me know at once, will you? And if you should see her, let me know where.'

Dutifully, each promised.

It had been a fair day at the shop, with cash sales of a little under a thousand pounds and orders for twice that amount. But for Deirdre, it would have been comparatively humdrum, however. It was after six o'clock before he left, and as he went towards the new Hart House where, by special arrangement with the new owner, he had a parking place, a young policeman appeared, a man whom he knew slightly. The man had been in the building, and was hurrying out, but he stopped at the sight of Mannering.

'Good evening, Mr. Mannering.'

'Hallo,' Mannering said. 'You're working late, aren't you? You were on duty this morning.'

'Had a nasty accident case and I've had to do a lot of checking,' the constable said. 'Er — do you mind if I ask a question, sir?'

'Go ahead,' Mannering said amiably.

'Did you notice a little red car — a Mini — standing opposite Quinns when you arrived this morning?'

Mannering said, thoughtfully, 'No, I don't think so. I saw one passing, though — coming from here. There were two men in it, I remember that they were very much alike.' Now that his mind had been forced to work the picture it produced was very clear indeed. 'One older man and a young one, who was driving, obviously father and son. Were they involved in your accident?'

'Oh, no! That happened weeks ago. No, but — well, they'd been opposite Quinns for about ten minutes this morning, before I moved them on. I just wondered if they were customers by any chance, or were watching some customers of yours. You can't be too careful, can you?'

'You certainly can't,' Mannering said. 'Very observant of you.'

'I'll keep my eyes open in case they turn up again,' the constable said. 'Goodnight, sir.'

'Goodnight.'

Mannering carried a picture of the young policeman's eager face as he drove his Aston Martin out of the space, keeping well to the left of the spot where the wall bulged but not thinking consciously that it was a common wall with the strong-room. He wondered why no one at Quinns had noticed the car if it had been there long enough to attract the attention of the policeman, but thought of the men and the red Mini was soon out of his mind. Deirdre Ballantine was back, right in the middle of it; he wished her anywhere but there, tried to get his thoughts back to the Kyoto discovery but could not. He kept seeing the pieces of the Ballantine jewellery. That necklace, for instance, dropped over the side of a ship and swallowed up by the ocean; or the brooch; or the tiara.

It was unthinkable, and yet he still felt sure that she had meant it. Certainly she had at the time.

It was equally unthinkable to allow her to do it. Her father might have the strongest aversion to charging her with what she had done, but there could be a very strong one for charging her and even having her remanded in custody so as to make sure she could not throw away the jewels.

What would Ballantine say now?

Soon — very soon — Ballantine would have to be told of the ultimatum.

There was, of course, the possibility that before long he would learn where the girl was, and she would probably have the jewels with her. Bill Bristow's old association with the Yard often proved invaluable, and this was one of the cases where it could be. The Yard's eyes were everywhere. Even without an official call for a particular man or woman certain officers could often keep track of individuals, and the daughter of a man like Ballantine should be well known. It was even possible that word would come by the time be reached his home in Green Street, Chelsea.

Green Street was now unique in London.

At one time it had been a thoroughfare of tall, narrow Georgian houses, not by any means the most attractive in the area, but pleasant enough. During the Second World War first a stick of high explosive bombs and then a shower of incendiaries had destroyed most of the houses, leaving only three standing; and in one of these Mannering lived. Over the years many new houses and some two-storey apartment buildings had replaced the rubble and waste land but the three Georgian survivals remained and Mannering and his wife still lived in the top flat of the southernmost one which, if one craned one's neck, had a view of the Thames. The far end of the street was a T-junction where smaller Georgian and some earlier houses were crowded, cottages cheek-by-jowl with Regency mansions. Mannering pulled into a parking place near his house and noticed a red Morris Minor next to a green M.G. The Morris reminded him of the policeman's story. He found the little cupboard of a lift on the ground floor, one of several concessions to modernisation. Perhaps because of the pepper attack he felt as if he had a cold coming on, for there was pressure behind his eyes and at the bridge of his nose again.

He stepped out on his landing.

Lorna might be upstairs in the attic, but before inserting his key he pressed the bell lightly; that way he wouldn't scare her if she didn't hear the key in the lock. As he opened the door, however, he heard her say,

'This will be John.'

So they had guests, and he was in no mood for pleasantries and small-talk. With luck, it might be someone whom they knew well, with whom small-talk wouldn't be necessary — someone with whom he could even discuss the events of the day. What he really wanted was a whisky and soda in his study with Lorna listening to his tale; why was it a man so needed an audience in times of stress?

She came from the drawing-room, telling him that these were special guests, not for the simplicity of study or kitchen. He forced a smile; and it did not have to be so forced because Lorna looked at her best in a loose-fitting two-piece suit of bottle green, her dark hair swept back from her forehead. There were some who said that in repose there was a look of sullenness about her, but he never agreed and at this moment her grey eyes were aglow, her often pale skin had a little colour; she had classic features for a woman.

'Hallo, darling!' He took her out-thrust hands.

'Hallo, sweet — I *am* glad you're early.'

'I haven't time for a teeny little pick-me-up before I sally into the fray, have I?' he asked, hopefully.

'Five minutes in the study while you tell me what's been going on,' Lorna said. 'I arranged it with our visitor, so I'm not simply waiting to throw you to the lions.' She led the way into a small room, oak panelled with panels which Mannering had bought from damaged fireplaces and church reredos over the years; on each hung a small Dutch painting, the mood of which suited this room perfectly. With its back to the window was a winged armchair, close to it a pouffe where Lorna often sat. By it was a small Elizabethan cabinet and he opened it to take out whisky and a soda syphon; gin and brandy were there also.

Lorna poured out, while Mannering said, very slowly, '*What* did you say?'

'I said you had five minutes in which to tell me what's been going on, darling.'

Mannering frowned, sipped, frowned again and said, 'Nearly everything.' His heart began to beat very fast, and he gulped down more whisky and said fiercely, 'Give me one guess and I'll name our guest.'

'Guess.'

'Deirdre Ballantine!' Mannering sounded almost triumphant.

'I wish you'd put some money on that,' Lorna said. 'The lady waiting with some anxiety to see you is Mrs. Anthea Ross.'

7

Lady Waiting

MANNERING NEARLY SPLUTTERED into his glass, he was so astounded.

Later, when he had had time to think, he realised that he should not have been so shocked but even then he could see no reason for having the faintest idea who the visitor would be. Now, he stood glass in hand, dabbing at his whisky-damp chin with a handkerchief, and his reaction took Lorna by surprise. He gulped two or three times before taking another drink more gingerly, put the glass down and stated with great clarity,

'I simply don't want to believe it. I don't really think it's true.'

Lorna looked at him levelly as she asked, 'What has happened, John?'

'In five minutes?'

'We really mustn't keep her waiting too long.'

'No,' Mannering agreed. 'No. What has she told you?'

'Very little,' replied Lorna. 'Mostly, that she knows there has been some serious trouble today between her fiancé, Sir Lucas Ballantine, and his daughter, but that Lucas won't tell her what happened and she needs to know if she is to help him.' Lorna raised her hands and eyebrows. 'Is that true?'

'The first part is true,' Mannering said. 'As for the second

— I can't possibly tell her. I'm far too deeply involved already, this would make my position utterly untenable. I simply cannot tell Mrs. Ross . . .'

He broke off, seeing a movement in the doorway, and Lorna also glanced round.

A woman stood there.

She was Anthea Ross, of course; she could hardly be anyone else in these circumstances, but he was taken utterly by surprise. Beauty he had expected; radiance would not have surprised him, or youth, competing with Deirdre. Beautiful she was and she might well be touched with radiance but she was subdued now; even sombre. She was not young, although it was difficult to judge the age of such a woman. Certainly she was in her forties, perhaps in her fifties. None of these things affected him, but the honey-brown colour of her skin did, for it gave lustre to her beauty.

She was a Negress.

She wore an off-white suit trimmed with dark green, and a turban of a hat — a hat of many beautiful colours.

'I hope you will forgive me for listening,' she said, 'and I hope you will change your mind, Mr. Mannering. Unless you do, at least two people and possibly three will be condemned to a life of unhappiness.'

Her voice was as rich as her skin.

* * *

It was not long, but it seemed a long time while Mannering stood and studied Anthea Ross, and she returned his gaze with similar frankness, similar appraisal. At last he moved forward and put out his hand. 'Mrs. Ross,' he said, 'I am very glad to see you, if more than a little surprised. Why don't you come and sit down in here, it's less formal? Sweetheart,' he went on to Lorna, 'will you hate me if I mention slippers?'

'Oh, darling, I forgot!' Lorna hurried out of the room as Mannering drew Anthea Ross forward and pushed a chair into position for her, on the far side of the fireplace. It was already getting dusk so only the evening light fell on her face.

'Do you like the gloaming?' he asked. 'Or would you like more light?'

'I am content like this,' she assured him.

'Perhaps if I light up one or two of the pictures...' He moved across and switched on two lamps, one glowing on the face of a priest dozing over a wine glass, another over two countrywomen obviously in earnest consultation. 'What will you have to drink?'

'Mrs. Mannering has already given me a tomato juice — I do not drink alcohol.'

'There are times when I envy you and times when I don't think I could live without it,' Mannering said. He moved to one of the panels and opened it to reveal a small refrigerator, took out some bottles of tomato juice and had poured out a glass by the time Lorna came back with a pair of suède slippers. He eased off his shoes. 'I've had quite a day,' he remarked, sitting back in his chair. 'Thank you, darling. Mrs. Ross, I can't imagine anything at all persuading me to tell you what happened between Lucas Ballantine and Deirdre. On the other hand I would go a long way to try to help even two of you to be happy. You couldn't be taking too gloomy a view, could you?'

'I don't think so,' she answered.

'Why do you think Deirdre is so prejudiced?'

'Isn't it quite obvious?' Anthea Ross countered.

'I don't want to think so.'

'I'm afraid it is,' Anthea assured him.

'A case of a child disapproving of a parent's mixed marriage — a reversal of the usual?'

'Yes,' Anthea said.

'Oh, *no*!' breathed Lorna.

'I really am quite sure,' Anthea averred, and for the first time she picked up her glass. 'It came with such a shock of surprise. We had known each other for years — my husband was an old friend of Lucas, virtually an uncle to Deirdre. In a way we were like sisters — perhaps more like auntie and niece — when I came to live in London. My husband was the Tali Ambassador to the Court of St. James,' she added with a touch of both dignity and pride. 'It was not until we talked of getting married that Deirdre changed. I can still hardly believe it.' The quiet voice held a note of sadness which could not be mistaken, but it vanished quickly and laughter replaced it. 'Lucas was even more astounded than I! Children can so easily astonish their parents, can't they?'

'Have you any children?' asked Mannering.

'Two daughters, both fittingly married to Tali diplomats in other African countries!'

Mannering chuckled. 'Will they approve or disapprove, I wonder?' Before Anthea Ross had a chance to answer he went on, 'Why did you come here?'

'Lucas told me that Deirdre had been to see you and he was coming, too. I didn't have a very happy afternoon,' she added wryly. 'When Lucas eventually returned, he was obviously upset, and he doesn't often show his emotions. He told me it was much better for me not to know what had happened, so I came to find out if you felt the same, Mr. Mannering.'

'I think that husbands and wives should make their own decisions,' Mannering said. 'Anthea — may I call you Anthea?'

'*Please.*'

'Anthea, are you sure there isn't another reason for Deirdre's attitude? Are you absolutely certain it's a question of colour prejuice?'

'Well,' replied Anthea, very slowly, 'I do distinctly remember her saying that she would rather see her father dead than married to a black bitch. I know she was angry at the time, but . . .'

'It did sound rather convincing,' Mannering finished for her. 'Do you want Lucas to know you've been to see me?'

'If you think it will help — of course.'

'I could tell him I think you ought to know what transpired,' Mannering pointed out.

'He's a very difficult man to persuade,' replied Anthea with a sigh, but the laughter was quickly back in her eyes — as it could be in Ballantine's and Deirdre's — and she stood up. 'But then, so are you! Thank you very much for listening, and if you can find any way to help I'll be for ever grateful.'

Soon, Mannering was seeing her into the lift.

Soon he was sitting back in the winged armchair, not unlike the one over the entrance to the strong-room at Quinns, a second whisky and soda by his side. Lorna was getting dinner, which would be a simple meal; she only had daily help and dinner-time help only when there were guests. He was over the surprise which Anthea had caused, and remembering her with a great deal of pleasure. Deirdre wasn't showing up at all well in any of this.

If he was being told all the truth.

It would be a long time before he forgot how completely he had been deceived by Deirdre, and he felt now as if he might be in the middle of some clever conspiracy. He was uneasy; but then he had been from the moment the pepper had been thrown at him; something was going on which he did not understand, but if he were to say so to Lorna, or to Bristow they would probably scoff and ask if he were feeling psychic! Lorna appeared, carrying a laden tray and set a small table in the panelled room; she had cooked minute steaks wrapped in bacon, some garden peas and brussels sprouts, and for dessert a deep dish of apple pie. She talking during most of the meal but not until they had finished did she demand,

'What will you do to help Anthea Ross, John?'

'Try to make Deirdre see sense.'

'You're not likely to,' demurred Lorna. 'Certainly not if she's as adamant as she seems to be. What was it you wouldn't tell Anthea?'

Mannering answered quietly, 'That Deirdre said she would rather throw the jewels into the ocean than allow Anthea to wear them.'

'And you still hope to reason with her,' marvelled Lorna. 'Darling . . .'

'Yes, my sweet?'

'Are you feeling *very* old?'

'Just about my age. Why?'

'I've never known you more unventuresome.'

'What should I venture?'

'You even need to *ask*,' scoffed Lorna. She was putting the dishes into a dishwater as he sat on a high stool and watched, enjoying the easy grace of her movements, and her quickness; it was surprising how often he could still find some aspect of Lorna that was new to him. 'The man I was once married to was a famous investigator.'

'Oh, *I* remember! A kind of private eye.'

'That's the word I was looking for. Don Juan — no, Robin Hood would sound much better. Do you remember the time when he actually robbed the rich to give to the poor?'

'I'll bet you soon cured him of that,' Mannering said feelingly.

'Oh, I did! But very soon he became a defender of lost causes, a man who would risk life and limb and fortune to help someone who was in trouble and unable to do anything about it,' went on Lorna. 'Of course I used to disapprove because he championed such peculiar causes. Why, he once fought a duel nearly to death on a roof for a woman who was half-demented.'

'And nothing like so attractive as Anthea Ross.'

'Exactly! She *is* beautiful, isn't she?'

'Easily the second most beautiful woman here this evening.'

'You're such a darling idiot, but so unperceptive tonight. How many times do I have to remind you that you've often risked life, limb and freedom for far less worthy causes than Anthea Ross?'

'Sweetheart,' Mannering said, moving suddenly and slipping his arms round her waist so that she leaned her head back on his shoulder and he could see her slender throat and the soft curve of her bosom. 'You aren't suggesting that I should go and find Deirdre and steal the jewels back from her, are you?'

'Not *steal*, darling. Recover.'

'There is a problem.'

'Such old, old age.'

'Of where to find her. However, Bill Bristow has friends who are looking for her and if they find out where she is they'll tell him and he'll tell me and then a visit might be worth while. I'm not sure, mind you, but if you ask very nicely.'

'Oh, John,' she said, catching his hands and pressing them against her, 'I'll ask just as nicely as I know how. Promise. I can't think of anything I would rather do at the moment than . . .'

'Go to bed?'

'Help Anthea.'

'Unnatural woman. Well, it may be that . . .'

Mannering, speaking lightly, but with an undercurrent of seriousness and acutely aware of her, heard the faint preliminary ring of the telephone a split second before it rang more loudly. He did not want to let Lorna go but the telephone was just out of reach, so he nuzzled her cheek for a teasing moment, then moved away and picked up the instrument. It could be anyone, of course; there wasn't the slightest reason to believe that it was Bristow.

But it was Bristow.

'John,' Bristow said, 'I know where Deirdre Ballantine is.'

There was a tone in his voice which warned Mannering that the simple statement wasn't all Bristow had to say, so all he said was 'Good' and waited. Lorna went out of the room and Mannering called, 'Listen in, Lorna!' Bristow paused for a moment as if to make what he had to say next more emphatic.

'I did ask you to be very careful of that young woman, didn't I?'

'Yes,' Mannering replied.

'I'm glad I did,' Bristow went on. 'She is living with a small group of young people in a kind of commune in Hampstead. Some are there all the time, some spend part of their time at home and some in this — er — establishment.' The emphasis on the word 'establishment' could well be a sneer. 'There are four houses which lead into one another very close to Hampstead Heath. Exactly what goes on I don't know but the Hampstead Division keeps the place under loose surveillance. It's known there is some pot smoking, and it's also known that although some of the couples are married there's a great deal of bed-hopping. However, the main cause for concern,' went on Bristow, only to pause for greater effect, and even changing the tone of his voice to one of deep significance, 'is that at least two of the men who go there have been inside for theft.'

Mannering felt as if he had banged against a brick wall.

'No doubts, Bill?' he asked.

'None. One is a Robert Tellman who held up a sub-post-office five years ago and has only been out of prison for a few months, and the other is Arthur Lee, who served three years for a smash-and-grab at a jeweller's shop in Tottenham. Both are ex-public school and come from good families — in fact all the people who live in or visit the place have good backgrounds.'

'Have you any idea how long Deirdre Ballantine has been going there?'

'Only vaguely. My friend at the Hampstead Divisional Headquarters said it was several weeks ago when she was first seen there.' After a pause he went on, 'John, it was always possible that she didn't go to Quinns simply to take away the family jewels.'

'Yes, I do realise that,' Mannering assured him. 'It's a fact that she didn't take anything else, too. I wonder . . .' he broke off.

'Go on,' Bristow urged. 'What do you wonder?'

'Whether she knows some of the men have records.'

'Whether she does or not she took the jewels there.'

'Can you be sure she didn't leave them somewhere en route?' asked Mannering.

'I suppose we can't be absolutely sure,' conceded Bristow, 'but where could she leave them?'

'Someone is going to find out,' Mannering declared. 'You wouldn't know if there's any chance that the place will be raided soon, would you?'

'There's no reason for a raid yet,' Bristow said.

'What's the address?' asked Mannering.

After a pause, Bristow answered heavily, 'I hope you're not going to stick your neck out, John. This girl simply isn't worth it.' When Mannering made no comment, he went on, 'It's known as Four-in-One, at the corner of Mill Street and Heath Avenue. It used to be a guest house before these people took it over.'

'It might be exactly the right place for Deirdre to work off her inhibitions,' Mannering mused, 'but it's a bad place for those jewels.'

'John,' Bristow said, 'all you have to do is lodge a complaint about what happened at Quinns this afternoon and the police will jump at the chance to raid Four-in-One. That's the quickest and easiest way to get the Ballantine jewels back, and you must know it. If you go along by yourself you could run into serious trouble. Don't do it, please.'

'I'll think about it,' Mannering said evasively.

'Just remember, Deirdre Ballantine isn't worth it,' Bristow repeated. 'That young woman is already well on the way to going bad.'

8

Risk

As Mannering stood up from his telephone Lorna appeared from the kitchen, coffee tray in her hands. Her expression told Mannering she had overheard everything on the kitchen extension. She put the coffee on the pouffe and stood looking at him, her eyes questioning. She was serenely lovely, and it was hard to judge what was going through her mind.

'Our Bill doesn't know Anthea,' Mannering remarked lightly. 'But he certainly thinks he does.'

'Yes,' Lorna said. 'I've been wondering — do we know her?'

'I know what you mean,' Mannering said.

'Have you decided what to do?'

'Nearly.'

She didn't press the question but sat on the chair where Anthea Ross had sat, poured out coffee and handed him his cup. It was very quiet up here; they were insulated against most traffic noises and had neighbours only on one side. Mannering was going through all that Bristow had told him, and remembering all he had seen on Deirdre that day. Suddenly, he asked,

'What impressed you most?'

'About Bristow's warning?'

'Yes.'

'I suppose the last words he uttered,' answered Lorna, and then she forced a laugh and spilled coffee in her cup. 'Oh, darling, why do I have to be so earnest about it all?' Her tone became much lighter. 'He said Deirdre was already going bad, and I wondered whether we — whether you — *could* change her direction.' When Mannering made no comment she went on, 'Anthea Ross was quite right about happiness. If Deirdre goes to the bad Ballantine will blame — well, not exactly blame, but you know what I mean — both Anthea and himself. That would be an ugly spectre all their married life.'

'If she married him,' Mannering pointed out.

'You mean she wouldn't take the risk of marrying him if she can't win Deirdre over?'

'I doubt if she would. Don't you?'

'Oh, bother it!' exclaimed Lorna, vexedly. 'Why did this have to happen? Darling, could you put it out of your mind for a little while? It may be easier to decide what to do then. Tell me what else has been happening, today, what exciting thing . . .'

'Sweet,' Mannering interrupted. 'I am going to see Deirdre, almost on your instructions. Or have you changed your mind?'

Lorna caught her breath, but did not speak.

'I doubt if she'll listen to reason, but she might listen if I tell her that if she doesn't give me the jewels I shall go to the police,' Mannering went on. 'At least it's worth a try. Half a cup more coffee, and I'll be off — and *no*, my darling, this is a job for me alone.' He laughed as he held out his cup. 'I've been in a hundred worse situations than this while you've waited at home asleep as often as not.'

Lorna forced a laugh, too, but she wasn't really amused.

* * *

He telephoned Ballantine's home but got no answer; he

might have to wait until morning before he could force the issue about reporting the loss. He was more than ever sure that he could not delay much longer.

* * *

A hundred worse situations, he reflected.

Times when the police had been on his heels and he had thousands of pounds'-worth of stolen jewels in his pocket . . . Times when all the evidence that he had broken a dozen laws seemed to crowd about him . . . Times when he had been within an ace of death . . . All of these situations had once been virtually commonplace to Mannering. For over ten years now he had been famous in London as an unpaid investigator . . . A consultant to the police and often in danger from criminals who would kill without a second thought.

Yes, there had been countless more dangerous situations.

But none had been with such a tenuous motive; and never had he gone quite so blindly ahead with no true idea what to expect.

Everything in this case had started so innocuously.

Perhaps the thing which most worried him was that Bristow was obviously so worried. What Bristow feared, of course, was that Deirdre Ballantine was being used by two men who had criminal records, or that she might already be conspiring with them. And that he, Mannering, might be held responsible for the loss, getting no payment from the insurance company.

He put the thought out of his mind as he drove past Four-in-One, at the top of a long hill road leading from Swiss Cottage. The windows and doors were painted in a riot of colours, what the moderns called psychedelic, but the grass was cut well, daffodils grew in profusion, a hedge was clipped neatly. The house was a mass of wooden gables and ledges, Victoriana at its most decorative, and each house had a small turret-room. The whole looked vaguely like a fairy castle or a picture of Disneyland, and there was nothing remotely sinister from the outside.

He drove round the corner, had to hunt for a parking place, squeezed in between a white Mini and a vintage green Bentley which dwarfed it, and walked back.

It was then twenty minutes past nine.

* * *

At twenty minutes past nine, in the Boater's Arms near Putney Bridge, Jonathan Cleff was drinking beer pint-for-pint with half a dozen men who had just finished a stint of overtime at a big construction site near by. He was dressed in a Harris tweed jacket and tight-fitting cavalry twill trousers and looked every inch the young officer. The building workers were in their working clothes, lusty, hearty men. One of them, Cleff had discovered by watching, was an expert with the pneumatic drill, breaking through concrete slabs and hard road surfaces in half the time taken by two younger men.

'And what do you do for a living, mate?' the driller wanted to know.

'I sell cars, chum,' answered Jonathan Cleff, which was half the truth; and it was what he always gave as his occupation.

'You don't need much muscle for that, just the gift of the gab.' The driller roared at his own joke.

'All you need for your job is muscle,' Jonathan retorted. 'Not a bloody thing more.'

'On me drill? Don't you believe it, mate, you've got to let the drill do the work, muscle don't come into it. Why even a child could do it *if* he had enough sense.'

'I've watched you and it looks like muscle to me,' said Jonathan.

'Okay, mate, come and have a go some time and see

where your muscle gets you,' the driller retorted. 'That's if you can take time off selling those cars of yours. You wouldn't stick it a day — not an hour, if you ask me.'

Jonathan looked at the froth on his beer and then into the little man's eyes.

'Is that a bet?'

'Five to one in quids you wouldn't last a day,' the driller offered with supreme confidence.

'Do I get paid as well?'

'Learner's rates, mates,' another man put in. 'Seven and a kick an hour on the drill, six bob navvying. Only don't turn up in those togs, you'd have to spend all your wages sending them to the cleaners!'

The others roared with laughter.

'You don't think I can do it, do you?' Jonathan Cleff remarked, and he drank half of the beer in his tankard before going on: 'When do I start? And where?'

'On the site, eight o'clock in the morning,' replied the driller. 'And if you just turn up I'll buy you a pint at lunchtime.'

'I'll turn up,' declared Jonathan, so quietly that there was nothing at all to reveal his elation. All he could see in his mind's eye was the bulge in the wall of the ramp in the garage at Hart House.

He stayed only twenty minutes longer, then went out to his red mini Morris and drove too fast towards Putney Hill. The sight of a policeman standing at a corner made him slow down. He mustn't be a bloody fool and attract attention for a while. During the next four weeks he had to be extremely careful. As he drove across Putney Heath towards Wimbledon Common and his shared apartment, he began to calculate. If he learned how to use that drill in ten days why not get the job done at Quinns in two weeks' time? Three, at the most. There wasn't any doubt that his father was slowing down, but it wasn't any use pushing him; not until he, Jonathan, could cut through concrete as easily as the little expert.

Jonathan turned into Cobbold Street as a girl came out of one of the gateways, a little young for him, perhaps, but she had what it took; my, did she have what it took! He needed a girl: not just someone to have fun with, a night or two or a day or two, but someone steady.

His father always discouraged his having the same girl for too long.

Yes — his father *was* slowing down!

* * *

Deirdre Ballantine sat in a reclining chair in a small room at the back of Four-in-One, looking at the jewellery, which was spread out on a small bed. She had never seen it displayed altogether until today, never as it was now. There were seventeen pieces in all, earrings to brooches, necklets to the tiara, rings to bracelets. The room was dark because there was only one small window, and the bedspread was of multi-coloured stripes in Indian cotton; nothing could have looked more ordinary.

But the diamonds and the rubies gave the room splendour. Light seemed to come from each jewel and to spread about the walls and the corners.

'My goodness!' she exclaimed. 'They're beautiful. They really are.'

She sat absolutely still.

The Four-in-One was less a communal than a community house with a communal kitchen, with cooking and housework done by the residents in part payment for rent. About a dozen couples and half as many single persons lived there permanently but there was also a shifting population of transients. She had been introduced here by a bearded youth with whom she had been infatuated until she discovered what his sex habits were like. The place had much less fascination for her these days but it was useful when she wanted to stay away from her father's house for a night or two.

From downstairs came the sound of guitars and banjos playing and even women singing harmony. From near by, a man kept bursting out laughing. In the next room a man or a woman was playing a haunting tune on a flute, but she was hardly aware of any of these, only of the white and red fire which was spread over the bed like a panoply.

And they were hers.

No one, least of all Anthea Ross, would ever wear them.

She moved forward and picked up a bracelet and slipped it over her left wrist; it seemed to set fire to her arm! She moved it about, slowly at first and then more quickly, watched the twists and turns of the hand and wrist, then caught sight of a reflection in a tiny mirror, and it held her spellbound. She put on the rings, two on her right hand, one on her left, and moved her arms about sinuously, as she imagined a snake-dancer would. The beauty and the fiery light were intoxicating her. She picked up the tiara and placed it carefully on the front of her head, and it glowed and glistened against the dark hair. Now every movement she made was caught by the mirror and the whole room seemed afire.

Footsteps sounded along the passage.

She felt a sudden panic, lest anyone should come in and find her wearing these, panic which flared as the footsteps stopped. She hadn't time to take off any of the jewels, hadn't time to do a thing.

A man banged on the door.

'You there, Deirdre?'

'I — yes, I — but you can't come in!' She pulled off the tiara and placed it under the bedspread.

'That is always the very moment when I want to,' the man called, half-seriously. He was Robert Tellman, rather an attractive six-footer and one of the permanent residents. 'You've a visitor, male, downstairs.'

A visitor here? Panic flared again, and she stopped pulling at the bracelet.

'*Who is it?*'

'He didn't give his name, honey, and I didn't ask him — no one asks questions at Four-in-One. I'll send him packing if you like.'

'What does he — is he *old*?'

'He wouldn't be flattered if I said he was.'

'How old?'

'Possibly forty-eight or so.'

'Then it's not my father, he's older,' she said with enormous relief. She took the rings off and put them under the bedspread with the tiara; it was strange but all the jewels seemed to have lost their magic, even their fire. 'I — I'd better come and see who it is.' She was unhooking the necklace now, which left only her earrings; in a way she felt that she was stripping herself. 'Ask him to wait . . .'

She broke off at an exclamation from Tellman, who exclaimed, 'What the devil are you doing here?'

'I wanted to make sure . . .' the other man began, and she would have recognised Mannering's voice anywhere.

But he did not finish.

Tellman said, 'Get the hell out of here,' and there was a scuffle of movement, the sharp sound of a blow which could have been fist on a bony chin. Panic-stricken again, she pulled off the earrings and dropped them on to the bed, then caught the corners of the bedspread together making a bundle of that precious collection. The thumping and the thudding continued outside. She bent down and thrust the bundle under the bed before spinning round towards the door and pulling it open. She expected to see Mannering in a terrible plight, he wouldn't have a chance against a man twenty years younger than he.

But Mannering was standing upright, unflurried and

unaffected; Tellman was on the floor, blood trickling from a cut lip, one eye looking pink and puffy. He was supporting himself with his hand against the floor and staring up at Mannering as if he could not believe what had happened.

Mannering turned to Deirdre.

'I'm sorry,' he said. 'I just couldn't take the chance that you wouldn't see me. May I come in?'

* * *

Mannering was sure that the girl was as scared as she looked.

He was far from sure about the tall man, whom he would not trust round the corner; he had given the other a lot of provocation and it would hardly be surprising if he attempted reprisals.

The girl stood to one side, without saying a word. He went in, aware that the other man was getting to his feet. 'Bob,' the girl said, but that meant nothing to Mannering at the moment. He went into the tiny room, little more than a cubicle and not remotely comparable with anything she would have at her father's house. Her hair was dishevelled and pretty; she looked attractive, flushed, obviously caught in an awkward moment, and she was breathing hard. He saw the bedclothes pulled at one side and the foot, and noticed what seemed to be a piece of striped linen under the bed. Apart from that, only her big handbag was in the room, lying on a rickety-looking bamboo dressing-table next to an equally rickety-looking wooden chair. Across one corner was a curtain, in another was a wash basin with a small wall cabinet above it. The walls were freshly painted, though, and gay.

Deirdre said, with a catch in her breath, 'You are wasting your time.'

'I may be,' Mannering admitted.

'How — how did you know where to find me?'

'I have a lot of friends,' Mannering told her.

'My father's been spying on me, and he told you!'

'No, Deirdre,' Mannering said quietly, reasoningly, 'he has no idea that I'm here. I asked a friend at Scotland Yard and it didn't take him long.'

She gasped, 'Scotland Yard! You mean you've told them I ...'

'No,' Mannering interrupted. 'I haven't told them yet. But you did commit a theft from my premises. I have every right and a lot of good reason to charge you with that and with assault. There's only one reason why I haven't: I don't want to hurt your father any more than he's been hurt. So I haven't been to the police. If I leave here without the jewels, though, I shall go straight to Scotland Yard and tell them the whole story of your visit to Quinns.'

She bit her underlip, but did not try to speak.

9

Menaces

MANNERING LISTENED INTENTLY for any sound in the passage, heard a creak and with a swift movement stepped to the door and pulled it open; no one was in sight. He turned back to Deirdre, who was now staring out of the narrow window; he was not sure but he thought tears were in her eyes. He waited for several minutes before saying,

'Where are the jewels, Deirdre?'

'I — I don't want her to have them.'

'Your family affairs are one thing. The safety of the jewels while in my charge is another. I simply don't have any choice, you know. And nor do you. My manager and others at Quinns can testify that you were there, your father doesn't have to give evidence . . .'

'Oh, take the bloody things!' she cried in a strangled voice. 'Go on, take them, give them to him, help him to hang them round her neck. But before you do tell him I'll never visit him again, I'll never go and see him again if he marries her. And make him realise that I mean it.'

'I'm sure you do,' Mannering said equably. 'Where are they?'

'Under the bed!'

He moved to the bed, sat on it so that he could grope and look underneath but at the same time move swiftly if she attacked or if anyone came into the room. No one did, and she stood still; whenever he glanced at her she was looking out of the window. He drew the bundle out with great care and raised it to his knees. It was hard to believe that anyone would handle such glorious gems in this way, and he felt a flash of anger towards her. The bundle was knotted, as a sheet containing a lot of dirty linen might be.

'You needn't open it! They're all there.'

'Thank you,' Mannering said simply, and went on to untie the knots. He did not open the bundle, simply drew the corners tighter so that they would not shake about and there was less risk that some of the gems would come loose from their setting. 'Deirdre,' he said. 'I hope you'll come and see me about this, before long. I still may be able to help.'

'Nothing can help, except preventing him from marrying that woman.'

'Well, if you come up with a good enough reason, who knows what might be worth trying,' he said cryptically.

Before she could speak, before she could even recover from her surprise at the remark, he went to the door, opened it very carefully, then stepped into the empty passage. He was not happy about the immediate situation, expected the man Bob to be round the corner at the head of a flight of narrow stairs.

No one was there.

He went down the stairs, once used by the servants, and leading down to the kitchen quarters. The music still sounded and a man was singing. He passed an open door and saw at least twenty young people sitting about by the walls, on low chairs or on cushions, and two men sprawled at full length on the floor, strumming guitars. 'Bob' wasn't there.

The clanging, metallic notes followed him along a passage to the main hall. The street door was on a latch and he stepped outside. For the first time he wanted to hurry, but he dared not allow the bundle to sway too much at his side. He remembered exactly where he had left the car, and it wasn't more than a hundred yards away. No one who offered any threat was in sight. He turned the corner, and saw only three young girls and, farther along, an elderly man and woman. The white Morris Mini had gone but the big old Bentley was still there.

He felt a surge of relief as he climbed into his own car, placed the bundle carefully on the floor beneath the seat next to him, and pressed the self-starter. The starter whirred but the engine did not start. That was unusual but he did not think beyond the fact that the engine hadn't fired, but at the second and third attempt there was no response.

That was when he realised that something was wrong; that this was neither accident nor coincidence. As he looked up he saw a small car swinging along the road and it pulled up in front of him, while on the same instant a big man climbed out of the Bentley; he must have been hiding in the back.

The man from the small car, who had parked so that he could easily get away, wore a stocking mask over his face.

The big man behind was 'Bob' — and it crashed upon Mannering that 'Bob' was short for Robert Tellman, a man with a record for robbery with violence. The small man approached from one side, the big man from the other, near the kerb. Mannering sat at the wheel of a car which would not start, with a hundred thousand pounds' worth of precious stones on the floor close to his feet.

'Bob' said, 'If you don't want to be hurt, hand those jewels over *now*.'

He held a small pistol in his big hand, inside the car where the driving window was down.

'Or shall I take them?' asked the little man, and he opened the near side door so that he had only to stretch out and take the bundle, turn, leap into his own car, and get away.

Mannering made himself *smile*.

And he made himself look into Bob's eyes although it was the other who could so easily take the jewels.

And he made himself say, 'You wouldn't get to the end of the street, Tellman.'

The use of the name seemed to strike like a physical blow; 'Bob' actually flinched and the other man said. 'What the hell!' The three girls passed, silently; the older couple was out of sight.

'I came to terms with the police,' Mannering went on, lying with complete conviction. 'If I could get these jewels back from Deirdre, whose family they belong to, no one would press charges, but if I failed then they would take over. There must be four men watching at this moment; there could be six or even more. *Look!* There's one, he . . .'

On the instant, Mannering leaned on the horn and it blared out, struck at Tellman's wrist so that the bone was banged sharply on the window edge, leaned in the other direction as the small man grabbed at the bundle and caught his wrist, twisted and yanked him into the car. All the time the horn was blaring on and off as he pressed or leaned against it, the three girls were gaping from a few yards away. The pistol dropped inside the car and Tellman backed away, gasping with pain, his injured wrist high in the air, his expression one of helpless anguish. Now Mannering began to play S.O.S. on the horn in a way that any police near by would recognise, and almost at once a uniformed policeman and a man in plain clothes came running. Tellman, catching sight of them, tried to run, but the pain at his wrist was too great. He staggered to one side and slithered down the wall of a garden. The other man's arm was twisted at an odd angle and he knew that if he tried to free himself a bone would break.

The two policemen came up, and on the instant the

plainclothes man exclaimed: 'Isn't it John Mannering?'

'Yes,' Mannering said, 'and never more glad to see you. I had just been to see a client with some jewellery and these chaps must have got wind of it. I hope I haven't done them too much harm.'

'Be difficult to do them too much,' the detective said sardonically. Then he broke into a laugh and looked thoroughly happy. 'I've been trying to get something on this pair for weeks. You know who they are, sir, don't you?... Robert Tellman and Arthur Lee... If you'll come along to the station and make a charge we'll cut the formalities as short as possible.'

'Just time enough to make my car go, I hope,' Mannering said.

* * *

Of the hundreds of people drawn to the scene of the attack on Mannering, by the noise or the police whistle or the sight of two men being handcuffed and later taken off in a police car, four came from Four-in-One. The news was carried back swiftly, spread among the crowd in the room where the guitars were briefly stilled, to the dining-room; everywhere. By ten o'clock, Deirdre Ballantine knew the story and had no doubt that Mannering had been the intended victim.

'Now there's a man who can take care of himself,' said a long, lean-flanked long-haired youth who told Deirdre. 'As for Bob and Arty, they'd loosened the distributor head in the other chap's car, they knew what they were about.'

'If they didn't they'll have time to learn while they're in jail,' a girl said, tartly.

Deirdre moved away from the group as soon as they began to play and strum and sing again. She went up to the little room which seemed even more bleak without the Indian bedspread. She stood by the window for a few minutes, tears creeping up and burning at her eyes, until suddenly she turned and flung herself on the bed and began to sob.

A girl in the next room heard her but took no notice. So many came here because the world outside had become so hopeless; and life did not seem worth living.

* * *

Mannering put his car into a garage rented from the tenant of one of the small apartment houses in Green Street, and walked to his tall house, whistling softly only just above his breath. He paused at the doorway looking up and down the street to make sure he hadn't been followed, then went up in the lift, still whistling. He had called Lorna to tell her he would be late, but not why, and was glad that he had, for the formalities had dragged on and on and it was now after midnight. He had also called Ballantine to say that the jewels were safe but had given no details. He touched the front door bell, and by the time he was inside the hall she was moving from the main bedroom, wearing a knee-length dressing-gown of rich red.

'Darling,' she greeted. 'You were wonderful!'

'Now what have I done?' demanded Mannering suspiciously.

'Recovered the jewels and out-fought two wicked criminals whose combined age is less than yours — *John.*'

'Yes, dear?'

'What's in that — well, what is it whatever you've got?' demanded Lorna.

'Oh, just a few trinkets,' Mannering replied lightly. 'How did you learn what I'd been up to?'

'A policeman at Hampstead telephoned Bill and Bill telephoned me. *Trinkets?*'

'Baubles,' Mannering declared. 'Come with me and I'll show you.' He carried the bundle with great care and led the way into the study. Against one wall was a Jacobean settle which he had converted into a safe many years ago, and it was bolted to the wall. By the side of this was a low table, and he pulled up Lorna's pouffe, then unfastened the bundle and began to take out the baubles.

First, came the tiara.

Next, the necklace with one of the earrings caught up in it.

Next again came a bracelet with a ring dangling; a pendant, a brooch, one magnificent piece after another. Mannering placed them carefully on the table where the dark polished wood made a perfect setting, then stood up and shifted the direction of one of the picture lights so that it fell upon Ballantine's collection.

The whole surface of the table seemed afire with the white heat of the diamonds and the red fire of the rubies. The scintillations seemed to grow in intensity, both to take life and to give life to the table. Everything else in the room fell away into shadows which were darkness; then the lights over the pictures seemed like tiny glimmers, a long way off.

Mannering stood with his arm about Lorna's waist. She was quite as affected as he, and the sight before them made their blood run faster and their hearts throb. They stood still for what seemed a long, long time, before Mannering stirred.

'I must put them away,' he said.

'John,' said Lorna.

'I'd love — some coffee. Even some biscuits. Perhaps a morsel of cheese.'

'John, do you realise that the table is exactly the same colour as Anthea Ross's skin?' Lorna's voice was husky, and she did not move, did not even take her gaze away from the fiery beauty so close to her. 'On her they would look . . .' Lorna stopped, groping for words.

'They would turn her into an empress,' Mannering said

with a low note in his voice. 'She would . . .' he broke off in turn, squeezed Lorna's waist lightly, and moved to the settle, taking out his keys, for this safe was a combination of key and electronic control. 'I'll put them in here and get them to the strong-room first thing in the morning.'

'It's almost criminal to keep them hidden out of sight,' Lorna remarked.

'Not while they're in my keeping,' Mannering said briskly. 'I want to be sure they're safe.'

* * *

David Cleff put aside the book he had been reading, a thriller of the classic whodunit *genre* and smiled across at Jonathan, who was skimming through some pop music magazines with a record-player close to him, playing softly; it was a Blues record with the drums sounding far off but played at magical pace. Jonathan grinned, prepared for what was coming, every-ready for praise.

'So you start learning to use a pneumatic drill in the morning?'

'*And* I get paid for it!'

'Don't forget you'll need to be out of the house by half-past seven.'

'I'll be on the site at eight o'clock on the dot.' Jonathan said positively. 'Er — Dad. May I ask a pertinent question?'

'When did you ever hesitate?'

'When I've driven a hole through the wall of that strong-room we do need a market for the jools, you know.'

'If you make your hole as certainly as I'll have my market standing by, we shall be rich men four weeks from now,' David replied cryptically, and he went off to his flat. Twenty minutes later, however, he tapped at the door of Jonathan's flat, to find his son setting an ornate looking alarm clock. Last minute visits like this were rare; they were not a demonstrative couple. David sat on the foot of his double bed, and gave a crooked smile.

'I know exactly how I am going to dispose of the loot,' he said lightly. 'Some, the easily negotiable jewels which can be taken out of their settings without losing too much value, we shall send to various banks for safe keeping — New York, Buenos Aires, Los Angeles, Cape Town, Sydney, any city where the gems can be turned into money quickly and we can open fat banking accounts.'

'How will you send them?'

'The way most jewellers in the trade send theirs,' his father replied. 'By airmail post. The risk is negligible, and we can get round to a dozen capital cities in a week or two, nothing will have to stay anywhere long enough to arouse suspicion.'

'*Very* nice work, but . . .'

'For the *objets d'art* and the jewellery which depends on its value because it's a part of a collection, we need a reliable buyer, and we can only get one quickly if we sell below value. So that's what we shall do. I have a buyer already interested, and there's only one problem.'

'Name it,' Jonathan said.

'We need a list of the goods for sale,' answered David. 'Otherwise the buyer will be buying blind or we shall have to keep the things on ice for a few days at least, and I don't want to do that.' He smiled into his son's face, seeing anxiety growing; that was one of Jonathan's weaknesses, he panicked at the threat of trouble or unexpected difficulty. On the other hand he was never frightened if he knew the odds against him.

'Then what are we going to do? How can we possibly find out what he's got in the strong-room?'

'It isn't very difficult,' David replied. 'We find out who Mannering insures with and we take a photograph of the list of items. We don't take anything away, we only need half an hour in the insurance office. You're going to learn to be a navvy and I'm going to learn to be an insurance clerk,' David finished. 'We've got plenty of time.'

If he saw the change of expression on his son's face, he did not refer to it, but got off the bed and went down to his own flat.

10

A Matter of Insurance

Mannering placed the tiara back in its velvet-lined case, peered at it for a moment and then closed the box and went out of the strong-room. Once the Regency chair was in position he unlocked the door and went to his desk. It was just after ten o'clock on the morning following the excitement at Hampstead, and for the first time he felt completely secure. The morning's post hadn't yet been put on his desk but there were some letters left over from yesterday and a list of appointments as well as a note of dealers who were in London from overseas. He refreshed his memory of these, and was about to ring for Bristow when the telephone bell rang. He lifted the receiver to hear Bristow saying,

'I'm not sure whether he's in, madame, but I will find out.' There was a click as Bristow put the incoming call on 'hold' and then his voice sounded stronger. 'John — I hate to tell you, but it's Mrs. Culbertson.'

Mannering smothered a laugh.

'I'll talk to her,' he said.

'I was afraid you would,' replied Bristow. 'John — I don't know exactly what happened but you did a remarkable job last night.'

'I had the breaks,' Mannering said mildly. 'Come and see me when the call's finished, will you?'

'Yes — at once . . . You're through, Mrs. Culbertson.'

Before Mannering could even begin to speak, almost before the call was through, the Australian woman cried: 'I've decided to have them! I couldn't sleep all night for thinking about them, I've never *seen* such green in all my life. And when I woke — I *did* drop off for a few hours — I knew I simply had to have them. You will do the very best you can for me over the price, won't you?' Then before Mannering could reply and with a refreshing burst of honesty, Mrs. Culbertson went on, 'But I mustn't plead poverty. I *can* afford them, one of my brothers just died and left . . . Oh, never mind, never mind. You *did* say thirty-eight thousand pounds, didn't you.'

'I would settle for thirty-five,' said Mannering.

'Oh, that's wonderful, absolutely wonderful! *Please* let me see them again this morning. And you will accept my cheque, won't you?'

'Gladly.'

'And I *may* see them?'

'You may take them with you,' Mannering said.

'Mr. Mannering,' she said chokily, 'I can hardly believe — but you know what a silly old woman I am! And I've no head for business, I should get them insured, shouldn't I?'

'I can keep them on temporary cover for a week, if we say you have them on option,' Mannering told her.

'Oh, can you? And *will* you? How wonderful! If I come at five o'clock this afternoon — goodo.' She rang off on the same note of excitement and Mannering smiled broadly to himself. It was at least three months since Edith Culbertson had first asked to see the Felisa Emeralds from the beginning he had been nearly sure she would eventually buy them. How wealthy was she? he wondered. And how much had she inherited from her brother? It was always good to know these things, for one day this woman would probably become a very big buyer indeed. He first dialled an insurance broker, named Diamond, arranged for the temporary cover 'while on approval for sale in the custody of Edith Culbertson', making a note for this to be confirmed. Diamond, one of the quickest men of his acquaintance, jotted down the details and said:

'I've been meaning to come and see you, Mr. Mannering.'

'To persuade me to increase my insurance cover, no doubt.'

'Either that or to have a more able-bodied nightwatchman on duty,' Diamond replied. 'May I come later in the day?'

Mannering scanned his diary.

'Three o'clock, if that's all right with you.'

'That will be just right,' said Diamond.

Mannering rang off and immediately dialled the News Editor of the *Sydney Morning Sun,* one of the biggest newspapers in Australia. The News Editor was an old friend whom he had been able to help in a variety of ways, and whom Mannering had come to know well when in Australia a few years ago. The deep voice with its unmistakable accent came on the line at once.

'Hallo, John, it's good to hear from you. Can I help you?'

'Thanks, Randy,' Mannering said. 'And yes, you can.'

'Just tell me how and it's as good as done.'

'You can find out how much a Mrs. Edith Culbertson of 401 Lowndes Square has just inherited from her brother,' replied Mannering.

There was a hiss of breath at the other end of the line, followed by a bark of a laugh. Then,

'You don't lose any time, do you?'

'I try not to.'

'Too right you try! He died two days ago and the amount of his estate won't be known for weeks, perhaps for months. But I can guess. I can also tell you he was a bachelor and was likely to leave his money equally to two sisters, one of them Edith.'

'How much you guess each one will inherit?'

The newspaperman said: 'Not less than twenty million pounds sterling between them, *after* all taxes. The old buzzard was nearly as rich as Croesus even before nickel and gold were found on his grazing land. Tell me, John, how did you find out?'

'His sister is quite excited,' replied Mannering drily.

'You bet she'll be excited! What she's going to buy?'

'A trifle,' Mannering said. 'So far! Thank you, Randy.'

'Always glad to help, John. I'll be in touch.' The newspaperman rang off, and Mannering put down his receiver slowly, leaned back in his chair so far that he could see the portrait on the wall above. Then he stood up, and went to see Bristow, who was on the telephone at his desk.

'No,' he was saying. 'Mr. Mannering has no statement for the Press.' He banged down the receiver, and glared up at Mannering before going on gruffly, 'That is the fourth newspaper to want to talk to you about last night's incident. I don't know what's the matter with me, John, I find it hard to be civil these days.'

'You are a bit touchy,' Mannering remarked, sitting in his favourite position on the Welsh dresser and looking evenly at the other man, whose features were drawn and who seemed tired especially about the eyes. 'Is there any trouble, Bill?'

Bristow hesitated, and then said in a flat voice, 'Not really trouble. I suppose I hadn't realised how much responsibility was involved here. Sitting on that strongroom is in some ways like sitting on a ton of high explosives!' He forced a laugh. 'And I was as worried as the devil about you last night. I shouldn't have let you go alone, but I wasn't sure you'd welcome me if I stayed on your tail, and — oh, the devil!' he exclaimed. 'It's a question of adjustment really, I suppose. How you keep your patience with old battleaxes like Culbertson I shall never know.'

Mannering gripped the edge of the dresser on either side of him, and said lightly,

'She's just bought the Felisas at thirty-five thousand pounds.'

Bristow's whole body went rigid, his eyes rounded, and his mouth actually dropped open. Slowly, very slowly, he began to shake his head as though this was more than he could believe. He had not fully recovered although he was looking much more himself when the telephone rang; he put a hand on it for a moment, letting it ring, and young Quartermain came hurrying, only to stop when he saw both men. Still slowly, Bristow lifted the receiver and announced,

'Quinns.'

At once, he said, 'A moment please,' and covered the mouthpiece as he said to Mannering,

'It's Lucas Ballantine.'

'Thanks.' Mannering took the receiver at once. Bristow wiped his forehead and moved away from the screen with Quartermain. Someone came into the shop as Mannering spoke into the telephone, 'Good morning, Lucas.'

'John,' Ballantine said. 'I was too shaken last night to tell you how grateful I was.'

'Oh, forget it. I . . .'

'I can't and certainly shall not forget it,' Ballantine said. 'And I won't take advantage of your goodness, but — is Deirdre all right? As far as you can tell, that is.'

'She's not running amok,' Mannering answered quietly. 'I think she's having a very rough time in several ways. She isn't behaving out of sheer devilry or animosity, she's being driven to it by some kind of internal pressure.'

'Not — not outside influences?' Ballantine sounded very eager to know.

'I haven't seen any evidence of it at all. Lucas . . .'

Mannering hesitated, before going on in a very positive voice, 'I think I could try to find out what's really goading her, and if I couldn't my wife could, but it would mean probing very deeply into your family affairs. You may prefer me not to.'

Ballantine said heavily, 'Anthea came to see you last night and Deirdre came yesterday. There isn't a great deal more for you to find out, is there? If you think you can help I would like you to try anything. It isn't now a question of pride, it really is a question of my whole future as well as Deirdre's and Anthea's. And I simply don't know what to do. The one thing I fear . . .' he broke off, as if in surprise; when his voice sounded again it seemed far away, and it was some time before he spoke directly to Mannering again. 'I'm sorry, John. I was going to say that the one thing I fear most is that Anthea may decide not to go ahead with the marriage. She may feel that will at least avert disaster.'

'Don't you?' asked Mannering.

'Disaster for whom?' asked Ballantine, more sharply than he had spoken this morning. 'For Anthea? I don't think it would be a disaster for her if we married without Deirdre's approval. For Deirdre? She's young, younger than she seems, in some ways. I couldn't live her life for her no matter how I tried, and the time will come when she will have a husband and a family of her own. It was never healthy that she should be so deeply involved with me — this could make, not break her. Or do you mean disaster for me?' Ballantine went on roughly. 'Is that the kind of disaster you think would be averted if Anthea decided not to go ahead with the marriage? Let me tell you, John, it would be the most disastrous thing in my life. I am not exaggerating. I have perhaps ten or fifteen good years of life left, and if they are to be good, if they are to be rewarding, if there is to be any happiness instead of the constant struggle against loneliness and depression and near-pain, then I have to share those years with Anthea. Deirdre has been wonderful but she needs a younger man as much as I need Anthea.' He paused but only for a moment; there was desperation in his voice as he went on. 'This situation can't go on. Deirdre won't come with me on official occasions where I can't take Anthea, and — well, Deirdre has to be made to understand how inevitable my marriage is.'

In the last few sentences his voice became difficult to hear, as if he were fighting for self-control, and before Mannering could comment the receiver went dead, and there was silence broken only by the imagined echo of the other man's voice.

In spite of that Mannering spoke as if the other were still there.

'All right, Lucas,' he said softly. 'I'll try to make her understand.'

* * *

Anthea Ross stood by Ballantine's side as he finished talking to Mannering, and placed a hand on his shoulder. Neither of them spoke; neither, in that moment was capable of speaking. At last Ballantine pressed her hand firmly and moved away from the telephone on his desk. On the desk, also, were photographs: of Anthea and of Deirdre, each in her way looking very lovely. Anthea picked up the picture of the girl.

'You can't reject her,' she said simply. 'You simply can't.'

'It isn't a case of rejecting her, but of her rejecting me. You must know that.'

'It can be a choice between us,' Anthea insisted. 'If you choose one you automatically reject the other.'

'I shall not reject you,' Ballantine said, very evenly.

'Bless you, darling.' Anthea faced him squarely now

trying to smile, trying not to sound too solemn. 'She won't stand aside happily for me, and she won't join us. I can't stay with you knowing that.'

'You've got to stay with me,' Ballantine interrupted roughly. 'It's no use, Anthea, I can't and won't go on without you. I *can't and won't.*' He took her hands and crushed them together and although the pressure must have hurt she did not flinch. 'You heard me talk to John Mannering. You heard me beg for his help. His, yours, anybody's, I want desperately to hold you both but if one or the other has to go it mustn't be you. Now do you understand. Now will you stop talking about leaving me? If you were to go it would break me.'

Anthea said very huskily, 'And can you mend, if Deirdre goes?'

'If she keeps on behaving as she has this last few weeks I don't want her,' he said fiercely. 'She isn't the girl I knew. She has changed—my God, to reject you on account of colour is unforgivable and unbelievable. I refuse to believe she will continue when she sees everything clearly, but whether she goes or not, you must stay. Do you understand me? I need you as I've never needed anyone in my life.'

'Lucas,' she said gently, 'didn't you once tell your wife that?'

Ballantine looked puzzled, even bewildered, as if he did not at first understand the question. Then he spoke, as if wonderingly, 'Tell Kathleen that I needed her? Good heavens no!'

'But Lucas...'

'Listen to me,' he said roughly. 'I've been in love, really in love, so that the thought, sight, sound of the other person can hurt or bring ecstasy just once. *Only* once. With *you.* I hadn't any idea what love was with Kathleen. I played a pleasant little romantic game. She was a very nice and charming woman, and most attractive, but she wasn't exciting. She and I seldom . . .'

He broke off.

He released her hands and then took her in his arms and held her very close to him; she could feel the beating of his heart and he could feel the swell of her bosom. He held her like that for a long time, and then said fiercely,

'There has to be a way of making Deirdre understand. There has to be.'

* * *

At that time almost to the minute, a very tired Jonathan Cleff was stepping away from the pneumatic drill which was now resting in its stand. His shoulders, chest, arms and thighs ached and his head seemed still to be bobbing up and down to the vibration of the drill. Dust smeared his face and made it like a mask, the cap he wore was covered with the dust. When he walked away it was stiffly, as if he had to force each leg in front of the other.

The foreman came up to him.

'Put a move on, mate, I owe you that pint,' he said. 'Don't want me to have to carry you, do you?'

'I — I can manage.'

'I'll tell you one thing, cully, you put more guts into that job than nine men out of ten. Half of the lazy so-and-so's give up inside the first hour. You did okay and don't you forget. You won't ever be as good as me, mind you. You've got to use your loaf, but you'll be good if you can stand the pace. And you can push your pay packet up to fifty quid a week if you know all the tricks. I'll put you wise, mate. Trust me.'

* * *

And at about the same time Robert Tellman and Arthur

Lee were standing side by side in the dock at the Great Marlborough Street Police Court, listening to a Hampstead Chief Inspector requesting a remand for eight days in custody. Neither man was represented, and neither protested.

11

Jack Diamond

At three o'clock that afternoon Jack Diamond entered Quinns.

He was a small, rather plump nearly bald man who had a babyish look about him; even his skin was pink and free from blemish and his clear blue eyes added to the illusion. He had a clear, well-modulated voice and a forthright manner, and knew his subject inside out. A specialist in all kinds of insurance which were slightly off-beat he probably handled more for antique dealers and jewellers, as well as private owners of these things, than anyone else in London.

Bristow had never met him until he went towards him at the front door. Two of the younger men were busy with customers, one showing a Greek ikon of remarkable antiquity, the third — Quartermain — had gone to value some *objets d'art* which were at a private sale in St. John's Wood.

Bristow introduced himself as they walked back to Mannering's office.

'This place always reminds me of a church,' Diamond remarked. 'Sometimes I think Mr. Mannering has an idea that it offers the same kind of sanctuary.' That coincided with Bristow opening the door, and was meant for Mannering to hear.

'That's why we have the strong-room,' Mannering said drily as they shook hands. 'Bill, don't go—bring up a chair.' He himself sat behind the desk, the others in front of it, and Diamond placed a small, flat, black brief case on his knees; they were pudgy enough for it to keep sliding off, so he moved it to the desk as Mannering cleared some reference books.

Mannering had a thick file open on his desk.

'You start,' he said.

'All right,' agreed Diamond. 'You have an overall or comprehensive cover at Quinns for two million pounds. Every item over one thousand pounds in value is specified by name and description. In addition you have a variable cover for goods in the strong-room which are not yours—either held for a customer or between sales. Does that agree with your figure?'

'Yes,' Mannering said.

'Humph.'

'Do you think we're under-insured?' Mannering asked Bristow, who was looking surprised.

'No,' the ex-Yard man said at once. 'If we're holding something here—like the Ballantine jewellery for instance—it's specified on value and automatically covered in addition to the stock, isn't it?'

'Yes,' answered Diamond. 'Mr. Mannering tells me what the value is, I issue a cover note, he pays me monthly. I keep the cover with various insurance companies as well as a special association with Lloyds. The system is virtually foolproof. We evolved it years ago. But two of the companies with whom I insure you aren't satisfied with the precautions any longer, Mr. Mannering. They don't think old Josh Larraby, at eighty, is a good enough nightwatchman, and they think someone else should be here at night and at week-ends.'

Mannering said slowly, 'The strong-room has always been considered secure enough.'

'Yes, and in some ways it still is,' Diamond told him. 'But thieves are becoming more expert and audacious. Two banks with so called impregnable strong-rooms have been robbed recently. And I have to say that I think you'd be wise, Mr. Mannering. There are some very clever and very strong gangs at work. Mind you, this isn't an ultimatum yet, and all of your coverage is good until the end of the year. I am pretty sure you'll have to take some steps if you want renewal, though, and I'm not sure you're wise to wait.'

Mannering looked at Bristow and asked again.

'What do you think, Bill?'

'I can't pretend I'm really happy as things are,' Bristow said. 'But then, you know, I'm very conscious of the responsibility anyhow. I may be too nervous. A local copper told me he noticed two men in a red Mini parked opposite for a long time yesterday. They were probably quite harmless where we are concerned but well, they may have been sizing the place up.'

Mannering thought: 'So he noticed: I should have realised he wouldn't miss them.'

He said, 'In effect, what you are advising is a man on duty from the time the staff leaves at night until the time we open next morning.'

'Yes,' said Diamond. 'And a good man who can take care of himself.'

'John . . .' began Bristow, but broke off.

'Go on,' urged Mannering.

'Well, I may as well be hanged for stealing a sheep as a lamb,' said Bristow with a grimace. 'John, Mr. Diamond said Quinns reminds him of a church and that you seem to think it's a kind of sanctuary. I know what he means. I'd never realised it before and I know you've always preferred not to have any security men here, preferring to keep the place empty at night, but it isn't empty with old Josh here. Quinns doesn't have a special dispensation. Thieves could kill old Josh Larraby as lief as look at him. You've been working this way for so long and the business has been growing so much that I doubt if you realise how much has changed. *That's* been my chief worry lately. I do think you've sufficient cover in insurance but I don't believe Quinns is impregnable, and I positively hate leaving old Josh here alone at night.'

Bristow's voice faded.

His eyes, clear grey, rather deep-set, were very steady and he did not look away from Mannering but he gave the impression that he expected Mannering to disapprove or at least disagree. Diamond sat very still and silent, realising that the mood of the interview had changed completely and this issue between Mannering and his new manager had suddenly come into the open. Mannering's eyes, hazel in colour, were as steady as Bristow's. He realised that this was a challenge to habit and tradition; that Bristow had been much more worried than he had admitted earlier. His brusqueness and occasional outbursts of temper might well be due to this anxiety.

To Mannering, it all came with the stunning blow of surprise.

He *had* taken the safety of Quinns for granted, and he could not seriously deny it; he *had* taken for granted the efficacy of the security arrangements which were a byword throughout the world. Why, even Hishinoto had said this was the one place where the unique Jimmu Tenno Treasure would be safe. He, Mannering, had ridden along on the waves of his own certainty; he had never really thought to doubt the sufficiency of the precautions.

But Larraby *was* an old man, and by most standards very frail. He had not wanted to retire even when he had, he had shared Mannering's feeling of the safety, almost the sanctity of Quinns; and that was nonsense. He realised that Diamond had deliberately said it reminded him of a church; that he, Mannering, had in fact considered it a kind of sanctuary.

Here were two men, one with a lifetime of police experience and who had investigated more jewel robberies than any other, who probably had second-hand knowledge of more safes, more strong-rooms and vaults than anyone else in London; the other with unique insurance knowledge, who knew the risks at least as well as and probably better than Bristow, both equally sure that Quinns was not properly protected.

And the Jimmu Tenno Treasure would almost certainly come here.

He began to smile, and on that instant Bristow — until then very tense — began to relax. He shifted in his chair and said mildly,

'And you both think a nightwatchman is the answer?'

'*I'm* sure the insurance companies will think so,' said Diamond.

'I don't think there's any way of making Quinns absolutely burglar-proof,' Bristow replied in a steady voice, 'but I'll sleep better at night if I know there's a man here. The strong-room and the shop . . .' he waved his hands—'well, I've realised you've known the risk, but Josh . . .'

'Bill, there's another aspect of this,' Mannering said. 'I'm not sure that I want a business so big that these precautions have to be taken. The place has grown out of all recognition, and that's what caught me napping.'

'Grown be damned,' interrupted Diamond. 'You've built it up layer by layer, year by year!'

'Let's say it's ten times bigger than it was and perhaps too big for a one-man business,' conceded Mannering. 'On the other hand, you're both obviously right and I can't go on as I am. Don't ask me why I didn't see it before: I simply didn't.'

'You'll get a nightwatchman!' Diamond exclaimed eagerly.

'As soon as we can find the right man,' promised Mannering, and he went on, thinking aloud. 'There are two on duty at Hart House, it might be practicable to tie in the security at both places.'

'I know one thing,' Bristow growled. 'I was a bloody fool to keep this business to myself. I should have talked to you about it before.' When Mannering didn't comment he went on. 'I think I can find the right man, but he'll have to *be* just right. The two chaps at Hart House might be the ones, as you suggest. Will you leave me to forage around, John and come up with suggestions?'

'Yes,' Mannering said.

'Is there any urgency?' Bristow asked Diamond.

'Sooner the better, obviously,' Diamond said. 'But my deadline is December 31st of this year.' He sat back in his chair, looking enormously relieved. 'And with this I'll fight for reduced premiums, too — I might save half the cost of a nightwatchman that way! Now, since I'm here, can we go through your inventory and check your list of items against mine?'

'Bill, this might be the best way for you to go through the contents of the strong-room,' Mannering said. 'No need for a physical check, but if Mr. Diamond reads from his list and you check against ours we'll make sure everything tallies. Better do it in here, I wouldn't mind some fresh air,' he added. 'It will help me to get used to the fact that I've been so wrong for so long!'

He left the two men together.

* * *

Bristow opened the insurance file and saw that he had a typewritten copy of each 'Schedule' of goods insured. Each schedule or list was with a different insurance company and, as he had known, some were with Lloyds. Each item was described in great detail, and as Diamond read out the details Bristow forgot what had just happened and lost himself with wonderment that there were so many treasures in this place.

The risk of discrepancies was only in items which had been sold, or returned to their owners, but in fact there was not a single discrepancy. The Ballantine jewellery was insured for a hundred and twenty thousand pounds, the Felisa Emeralds for forty thousand.

The more he saw of this the more relieved Bristow was that there was going to be a nightwatchman. And the more certain he was that, even if it took some time, they must find the best possible system of security.

* * *

Mannering walked along Bond Street, then turned into Savile Row and into the end of the Burlington Arcade, with its tiny shops, so many of them exclusive, each one with a style and a quality which made it unique. He was still feeling rueful, even a little breathless. He *had* been blind for a long time but that did not make the shock of seeing the truth any less. Gradually, however, the situation fell into perspective. One thing which helped was Bristow's deep concern for Josh Larraby; another was the thoroughness with which both Bristow and Diamond considered his, Mannering's affairs. Both were warming. Far less warming, and in fact chilling, was the realisation that Quinns had grown so big that it was too large to be properly controlled by one man, and wrong to place so much responsibility on a manager, such as Bristow. The business had grown almost without his realising it, yet trying to give every piece which came in and every customer or colleague the proper personal attention was becoming more and more difficult. Add an affair like the Ballantine one and it could become impossible. He had no doubt that his preoccupation with individuals had blinded him to the security problem.

That was why he had told Bristow he thought Quinns was getting too big.

It had been an immediate reaction, a way of defending himself aggressively but — wasn't it true?

Did he really want a business which had to be handled by others? Wasn't half of the attraction the fact that he had both time and opportunity of taking an interest in individuals such as Edith Culbertson? And he had to squeeze time for her; how many did he neglect?

He stopped abruptly at the window of an art gallery, hardly able to believe his eyes. He actually backed away and bumped into a man, apologised and heard a man say, 'Surely,' in an American voice, but he was not aware of how curiously the young American looked at him, he was intent only on the portraits in the window. There were seven in all, too many for the small space, each one beautifully painted, and four of the subjects — all women — known to him. But the thing which had pulled him up so sharply was the small sign at the front of the window, reading:

Exhibition of Portraits by
LORNA MANNERING, R.A.

He had not known Lorna was holding an exhibition here or anywhere!

Yet here were some of the best examples of her work, each painted up in the attic studio above their flat at Green Street, or at least finished there even if the sittings had been somewhere else. Inside the shop were other portraits of both men and women, every one by Lorna, each having her quite inimitable touch. She had a gift of catching the life of her subjects; it was as if they were breathing.

Two men whom he did not know, were talking inside the shop.

Mannering went slowly on, looking at but not really seeing any of the other windows. *He had not known of the exhibition.* That meant Lorna had not told him, and he was nearly sure why: he was always so preoccupied, wanting to discuss what was happening at Quinns, asking only perfunctory questions about what she was doing herself.

'Good God!' he exclaimed when he reached Piccadilly.

And he had first been concerned because he was neglecting customers like Edith Culbertson!

He glanced at his watch; it was only ten to four. He glanced up, saw several taxis with their signs lighted, hailed the nearest and said, 'Green Street, Chelsea,' and when he reached the house asked the driver to wait, and hurried in. But it was an abortive journey, for Lorna was out. He went up the ladder into the loft and saw several half-finished portraits on easels, and other canvases in various stages of preparation with their backs to the studio, which was redolent with the odour of paint. He resisted a temptation to leave a note, went downstairs and was back at Quinns at a quarter to five.

Diamond had gone.

Bristow looked years younger.

So did Mrs. Culbertson when she arrived, a few minutes before five, with the cheque already written, carrying an old and worn leather brief-case to take away her treasures. She said hardly a word during the brief formalities but there was a suspicious glistening in her eyes when she left Quinns, and Mannering watched her walk along Hart Row in her shapeless old tweed suit, looking as if she hadn't the proverbial two pennies to rub together.

At a quarter to six everyone else had gone except Mannering and Bristow; this was the first time they had been on their own since the decision about the need for extra precautions. But Mannering wasn't thinking about a nightwatchman then; he was wondering how much thought Bristow had given to his remark that he wasn't sure he wanted a business so big that such precautions had to be taken.

For he might have relieved Bristow of one anxiety, only to burden him with another.

12

Bristow's Offer

Nothing at all in Bristow's manner suggested that he felt any new burden. He really did look younger and more relaxed; he even moved across to the chair over the strong-room, leaning back in it while clasping the arms, and saying with great confidence,

'John I'm sure you won't regret what you've decided.'

'I'm pretty sure, too,' Mannering admitted. 'It will take a lot of getting used to, and I do wonder whether Quinns hasn't outgrown me, but . . .'

'Quinns will never outgrow you,' Bristow interrupted, as if without a doubt in the world. 'You're synonymous with it, John. There may be some changes and you may even give your manager more authority sometimes but . . .' He became momentarily wary, as if wondering whether that had gone too far, but when he saw Mannering smiling he went on, 'Every day I'm here I learn a little more about the business and about you, but today was a red-letter day. Do you know what Diamond told me?'

'What did Jack Diamond tell you?'

'That if you put a value on any piece of jewellery, any painting of any *objet d'art* or antique, any insurance company will accept the valuation. So will every reputable dealer or auctioneer. I always knew you were unique but not until today *how* unique.'

'So unique,' Mannering said with feeling, 'that I didn't know Lorna had an exhibition in a gallery in Burlington Arcade. I saw it by accident this afternoon.'

'If I know Lorna that will worry you much more than it will worry her,' Bristow declared, in a tone which carried its own reassurance. 'But John, you do need a break. Not simply a holiday but a few weeks when you needn't concentrate so much on Quinns as you have been doing.' He frowned as he stared at Mannering and then appeared to change the subject abruptly. 'You know I've a son in Australia, don't you?'

Surprised, Mannering said, 'Yes — and I seem to remember you were going to take your wife out to see him.' *Could* Bristow be about to announce that he needed a holiday, too? The timing would be most unlike him but he might believe that he should get everything over at once.

'I was there two months before leaving the Yard,' Bristow said. 'I don't particularly want to go again for a few years anyhow. But my wife would love to go and spend three or even six months with the boy and his wife, while in a few weeks' time the lease of our flat comes up for renewal and I don't want to pay the extra rent the landlord wants.' Bristow gave a sudden grin: 'Quite a chapter of events, isn't it? If Ellen goes to Australia, I could nightwatch here while looking round for a smaller flat in the heart of London. There is a spare room up in Josh's place if we moved some of the antiques around a bit, and working this way would suit everybody's purpose until we decided the best thing to do. And if I were here night and day you wouldn't mind being away more, would you?'

After a long pause, Mannering opened a cupboard in a corner behind him, took out whisky, soda and two glasses, and began to pour out.

'You're not making this Australian business up just for my benefit, are you?'

'Call my wife and ask her,' Bristow challenged.

'No, I'll take your word for it!' Mannering handed him a whisky and soda. 'And if you're really serious...'

'I couldn't be more so,' Bristow assured him.

For Mannering it was a strange day, a day of quick decisions; and when he tried to rationalise them later he came to the conclusion that much must have been hovering on his subconscious for a long time: the need for changes, latent awareness that things could not go on as they were. That evening, when he talked things over with Lorna, and at this moment in the office he felt the same sense of inevitability, and the same sense of gratitude that Bristow was not only here but willing to do what he suggested. For there was no one in the world for whom he had a warmer regard and a deeper respect.

'Then let's drink to it,' he said.

And they raised their glasses.

* * *

'My God!' gasped Jonathan Cleff. 'I'm exhausted.'

'You've put a bit too much into work today,' his father suggested.

'*I* want to get the big job over,' Jonathan said, his physical fatigue making him forget the caution he knew was necessary with his father of the raid on Quinns. 'I'll tell you one thing that will please you. I've learned where I can get a pneumatic drill which will work from electricity — all the pressure is inside the drill, you don't have to have a compressor. How about that?'

'Wonderful!' applauded David. 'And now you want a long soak in a hot bath.'

'That is precisely what I'm going to have, after you've poured me a whisky and soda.' Jonathan sprawled back in a big chair in the room they shared, outer clothes off, bigger and brawnier than he appeared to be when dressed. He watched his father pouring out, and, as he took a glass, asked roughly, 'Dad, what would stop you from doing this job at Quinns?'

'Nothing,' David Cleff answered quietly.

'Absolutely nothing? Are you sure?'

'What's on your mind, Jonathan?'

'One of the men on the construction job was talking this afternoon — it's amazing how some of them do talk, no wonder these big buildings take so long to put up! His last job was nightwatchman at a big store. He gave it up because it was so lonely. What would happen if there were a nightwatchman at Quinns?'

David Cleff answered, 'We should have to cope.'

'You wouldn't let him stop us?'

'No, son,' David said very quietly. 'I won't let anything stop us. The more I think about the raid on Quinns the more it means to me. I was with another antique dealer today and we talked about Quinns.' The older man's voice was very hard and his face was set and bleak. 'It will be my last job, and so the last job we shall ever do together. It is going to succeed and nothing is going to stop us. Not even this.' He picked up a copy of the London *Evening News* and pointed to a small paragraph on the front page, which read:

Nightwatchman Murdered at Bank

Then sharply, David asked, 'That's what really worried you, wasn't it? You'd read that.'

Jonathan said gruffly, 'Yes. Mind you, there was this chap, but if I hadn't read that story I wouldn't have thought twice about it.'

'Jonathan,' said his father, 'we are going to raid Quinns. I have all the overseas banks lined, up, I shall write to them one after the other, say I'm making a business trip and will want to come and see them and meanwhile am sending some documents for their safe keeping.'

'You've gone that far!'

'Yes. I have also discovered that Mannering doesn't deal direct with insurance companies but through a broker named Diamond, and it should be much easier to get the information we need from a single broker than a large insurance company. I'll tell you something else I've done,' he added, his gaze still fixed very intently on his son. 'I've arranged to get passports under different names, in case there should ever be suspicion of us. When we travel we won't go as father and son, we'll travel as business associates.'

'My God, you're thorough!'

'Jonathan,' his father said. 'I have been dreaming of a raid like this for many years. I am not going to allow anything to stop me, especially not your impatience. We need every minute of these four weeks to prepare, and we're going to use them. We've had three days already, it's surprising how soon the time will go. *Now* I'll drink to success, if that is what you wanted your whisky and soda for.'

'I wanted that as a pick-me-up,' Jonathan said, 'but I'm damned if I need one now! Success!'

'Stop at nothing,' his father toasted.

* * *

'Well, dear,' Mrs. Bristow asked her husband, 'are you sure you'll be all right living at Hart Row?'

'Even more all right than I'd expected,' Bristow said. 'I didn't know that old Josh has a sister or a cousin or something in the country near Oxford. He'd love to spend the summer with her but didn't want to let John Mannering down. So I shall have the full use of his flat, and be as snug as a bug in a rug.'

* * *

Lorna's eyes positively danced when Mannering told her what had been decided.

'Darling, you've needed something like this for *years*,' she said warmly. 'It's absolutely wonderful. And now I dare tell you that I've a summer exhibition in San Francisco, and even dare hope that you'll come!'

* * *

Mrs. Culbertson, alone in her large apartment in one of London's loveliest squares, surrounded by antiques and *objets d'art* most of which she had bought from Mannering, dressed for a solitary dinner which would be sent from a nearby restaurant in her very finest evening gown. When the waiter had brought the meal, in a heated tray which could be carried like a suitcase, she told him,

'This is an anniversary I always celebrate on my own.'

'Poor old soul,' the waiter thought. 'She's as lonely as hell.' He went out of his way to be pleasant, accepted her ten shilling tip gratefully and went out. When he had gone, Mrs. Culbertson hurried to her bedroom and stood in front of a tall mirror. The dress was a dark gold colour and so beautifully cut that it graced even her ungainly figure, and there was a glow of colour, excitement in her eyes. She studied herself for some time, then opened a drawer in a big chest and took out the Felisa Emeralds.

She stared down at them, as if hypnotised.

Slowly, she took one piece, a necklace, and placed it in position; placed earrings and rings and bracelets, too, until every piece in the collection adorned her. She studied herself in the mirror, moving to make the emeralds glimmer, then at last went to the other room and began her meal.

Only two doors away, thieves were looting an apartment nothing like so full of treasures as this.

* * *

Anthea Ross and Sir Lucas Ballantine had a quiet dinner alone at Ballantine's house. Ballantine had asked the police to watch for Deirdre but there had been no news of her since she had left Hampstead. Whatever Ballantine might say, the silence from his daughter dimmed the spirit of them both.

Anthea thought, I simply can't stay with him while she is like this.

Ballantine thought, I must be more cheerful or I shall drive her away.

* * *

Deirdre Ballantine was already tired of the tiny room; tired of the ceaseless strumming from below; tired of the fact that every man who lived here seemed to think that she had come simply to share her favours with him. Strangely, one who hadn't was Bob Tellman, and she had seen a paragraph about his remand, and Lee's in the *Evening News*. When she had paid her first visit here four weeks ago it had seemed a heaven on earth compared with the strained conversations at home; the engagement between her father and Anthea had caused such an upheaval in her life that all she had wanted was escape from it, and Four-in-One had seemed exactly the right place to escape to.

Now, she knew no one here to talk to; no one to whom she wanted to talk. She would almost as lief be at home.

As it was she felt she could not stay in all the evening, and at least no one attempted to keep her in, one could come and go as one pleased here, all one had to do was pay a modest rent. She walked briskly to the Pond, not sure where she would go from there, saw a bus, got on it, and found herself heading for Swiss Cottage and the West End.

Before she got off the bus, she knew where she wanted to go: to Quinns, to the place where the jewels were.

They haunted her; and the fact that they would soon be Anthea's to wear still tore at her in a way she did not really understand. At Oxford Street she walked through the maze of narrow streets and alleys to New Bond Street, and at last reached Hart Row. She walked along it, anxious not to show too much interest in Quinns, pretending to look at the carpets in a brilliantly lighted *salon*, or in the milliner's shop, which was not lighted. Quinns was in darkness at the front, but there were lights inside so that any movement would be noticed; and the police patrolled this little street regularly.

She passed a young man.

She did not notice him at first, except that he was walking from the big new office building. She did not notice when he turned to look at her. She went into the courtyard of Hart House and then turned back. A huge wall now hid the old roof and beams of Quinns but she knew that the shop was an Elizabethan gem. She turned and walked back, and noticed the youth for the first time: that is, she saw that he was nice-looking and well-dressed. He was now studying the carpet *salon* while she was on the other side.

She reached the corner.

She was *very* lonely.

She knew the danger and the folly of pick-ups, but she hadn't spoken to a soul since she had seen Mannering the previous night. Just along Bond Street was a jeweller's shop with some silver in one window and gold in another, each under spotlights. On the opposite side of the road was a red Morris Mini. She paused and looked into the window. Her heart began to thump. The young man appeared at the corner and came towards her, slowly, not boldly. She did not glance towards him. He stopped by her side and said in a hoarse voice,

'You wouldn't care for a drink, would you?'

She looked at him as if taken by surprise, and she liked what she saw. She didn't answer at once, which was silly, for she might drive him away.

'There's a decent hotel bar not far along,' he said. 'The Westbury. Do you know it?'

'Yes,' she managed to say.

'*Do* come and have a drink.'

She decided, suddenly, that there could be no harm in accepting the invitation; that she wanted a drink, and in fact she needed a meal! And this man looked pleasant and rather shy.

'Thank you,' she said.

'You *will*?'

'Yes — thank you.'

'Oh, that's wonderful!' he said warmly, and moved quickly to join her — and then winced. 'Oh, lor — I'm so stiff. I had an unexpected run today and I'm out of practice!' He didn't take her arm or touch her, just escorted her across the road, past the little red car, round the corner and into the Westbury Hotel. On the bar were some little sausages and meatballs and she could hardly keep her fingers off them.

'What will you have?' he asked, and pushed the dish towards her. 'Try one of these. They're good.'

* * *

Jonathan Cleff thought, She's a good looker, and she's got what it takes and she'll be a pushover if I handle her properly. I've seen her before somewhere.

But he could not think where.

13

Where?

DEIRDRE LIKED HIM.

He had a pleasant manner and a voice she rather liked although she was nearly sure it wasn't public school. When he said he was a car salesman, that seemed to fit him. There was no doubt that he was very stiff; now and again when he moved quickly or bent down to pick up something he'd dropped, he actually winced.

'That must have been a long run you did today,' she remarked.

And she wondered, idly, even amusedly, whether his stiffness was the reason he did not ask her to go to bed with him. Of course he might simply be 'nice', there were plenty of nice young men but something about him suggested that he was nothing like as naïve as he had tried — at first — to make out. One thing was certain: she felt more herself than she had for days, perhaps for weeks. She had made quite a meal of snacks and sausages, and no longer felt weak and ravenous. She wondered what he would suggest next; surely something.

'To tell you the truth,' he said. 'I didn't run at all.'

'Oh. Someone just beat you up,' she said lightly.

'No. I — er — oh, I may as well be honest!' He looked honest, too, but she was wary, her experience told her that was an ominous opening gambit. 'I haven't sold many cars lately and I took a labouring job to see whether I liked it. You'd never believe what job I was given.'

'Tell me.'

'A pneumatic drill!' he exclaimed. 'I still seem to shake all over. As a matter of fact that's really why I was so timid when I spoke to you tonight, I wasn't really sure I could lift a glass to my lips.'

'In which case I'd assume you were an alcoholic or on pot,' she said.

'That's *exactly* what I feared you would think. As it is, I managed quite well. Except . . .' he hesitated, putting his head on one side and looking at her crookedly.

'Here it comes,' she told herself. 'Will I be patient with him if he . . .'

'That I have to get up at seven in the morning for the job,' he said.

'Good gracious!' she exclaimed.

'Don't you ever get up that early?'

'Often. I — I mean, are you going on with the job?'

'Certainly,' he replied. 'For a week or two, anyhow. The foreman, an Irishman about four feet ten, says there's nothing like proficiency with a pneumatic drill to make a man a man! And if there is anything I love being, it is a man!' His eyes mocked her. 'May I drop you somewhere? And *please* may I see you again tomorrow night?'

She said, smiling, 'If you'll drop me at home I'll be grateful, and if I can get here tomorrow about nine o'clock, I'd love to.'

'Promise?'

'Not a promise. But I'll try.'

'You couldn't possibly not want to see what a pneumatic drill does to a man! If not tomorrow, Friday?' When she didn't answer he went on firmly, 'I shall be here at nine o'clock each night until you come. That *is* a promise.' His tone changed and he looked at her as if he were suddenly troubled. 'Are you all right, Dee? Did I say something to upset you?'

'No, nothing at all,' she answered quickly. 'You've been charming and I really will try to come.' But she knew that the life had gone out of her voice and her face, and she also knew why.

She had asked him to take her 'home'.

For a few moments she had forgotten the situation at home, he had lifted her out of herself completely, but now she came up against the sharp realisation. She hated the thought of going back. There was a kind of fate about it, however, and she went out with him and round the corner and across the road, to the red Mini car. She was so utterly preoccupied with her own problems that it did not cross her mind that she had actually seen him once before, when he had been sitting in it with another, older man. She had not the slightest recollection of that.

'Where to?' he asked.

'Twenty-eight, Breckon Square,' she answered. 'Please. Do you know it?'

'Just off Breckon Street in Knightsbridge?'

'Yes, that's right.'

'I live in the Wimbledon area,' he said, 'so I have to pass close by your place.'

He got out of the car to open the door for her, despite her protests but did not come to the front door and did not attempt to kiss or hold her. She still wasn't sure whether this was because he ached so much or whether he thought it was wise; whether it was his way of 'handling' her. It was never possible to be sure with men, and one thing she owed to her father was some knowledge of the tricks they would play to get their own way.

She stood on the porch watching the rear light as it neared the corner and then disappeared. Only the tall street lamps were on, with lights over one or two doors and at a few windows. She had not been able to see whether there was one at her father's study window, above the porch: the little car had been difficult to see out of. She still hesitated. The last thing she wanted was a confrontation with her father and there was nothing to stop her from walking to Knightsbridge where she could get a taxi; or she could book in at a nearby hotel, it wasn't really late. For a fleeting moment she actually thought of going to see John Mannering.

For the first time, she wondered why Cliff—he had told her that his name was Clifford—had been in Hart Row.

Then she thought: He'd been watching me, of course! And she smothered a laugh.

It was that laugh, indication of a much better mood and one in which she felt sure she could control herself whatever happened, which made her decide to go indoors; she told herself that if her father did ask questions or start to reason with her she would simply turn round and come out again.

She put her key in the lock, turned, and pushed; the door opened. The hall light was on, low, as it was always kept if she were expected home late. There was no sign of anyone down here and no one on the staircase or the landing. The front door opened on to a wide hall off which the staircase led and alongside the staircase was a passage leading to the kitchen quarters. All of the living-rooms were on the first floor, the bedrooms on the two floors above.

She went upstairs and saw her father come out of his study; very likely he had seen her arrive. She almost screamed: *Don't talk, don't reproach me.* He did not come to her but stood in front of his door, subdued light behind and in front of him. She could not fail to see how handsome he was.

'Hallo, Dee,' he said; and that was her family nickname,

'Long Legs' was one he used exclusively. 'It's good to have you home. Do you need anything?'

She said : 'No. I — I'll just have some tea in my room.'

'I made sure there was some milk there,' he said, and at last moved forward. This was the crux of her homecoming, the moment which might break it or give it hope. He kissed her lightly on the cheek and said : 'Good night,' and pressed her hand and turned back to his room.

There were tears in her eyes when she reached her own, found a tea tray set ready, a nightly custom which had not stopped because she had been away. But the tears had dried by the time she made tea and drank it. She was thinking a lot about Cliff.

Stiff Cliff !

* * *

'Tonight of all nights,' groaned Jonathan Cleff, who had long used the name Clifford for his dates and, when it became necessary to use a surname, said that he was really John Clifford, and this explained away the initials J.C. on his handkerchiefs, ties and sometimes socks and shirts. 'I had to meet *the* girl.'

His father laughed.

'And couldn't you perform?'

'I had the sense not to try! Hey, Pop.'

'Yes.'

'She was a real humdinger.'

'I thought yours always were.'

'But this one really *is*,' Jonathan insisted. 'There's no reason why I shouldn't entertain her, is there?'

'Here?'

'It's cheap and comfortable here,' Jonathan said, reasonably, 'and I can take her to dinner in Wimbledon or Putney for half the price I can in the West End.'

David looked at his son's eager face.

For his part, he wanted no distractions until the Quinns job was over; there were two women in Soho to whom he could go for amusement and pleasure, but they would hardly be distractions. Jonathan was different, and it was not simply a matter of age. Jonathan was a more restless character, he continually needed fresh interests, needed to imagine himself in love, needed conquests. If he became involved with a girl, and did not bring her here then he would probably stay out into the small hours and generally exhaust himself. And they had an understanding that if either was to have a guest, for an hour or two or for a weekend, the other kept in his own flat. It had worked very well for several years and there was no reason why it shouldn't work well now. In fact, David Cleff argued with himself, if Jonathan had a 'steady' for the next three weeks it might help him to be patient during what was for him to be a long wait.

All of these things passed swiftly through his mind; Jonathan had no time to wonder what he was thinking.

'I think it's a good idea,' he said lightly. 'But make sure you know who she is before you bring her, won't you?'

'I will,' Jonathan promised. 'I did very well for a start — I call her Dee.'

His father laughed, and said: 'Good night — Clifford!'

He had no idea where Jonathan had met the girl, and Jonathan did not breathe a word. He himself suffered an almost hypnotic pull from Quinns, and he simply had not been able to keep himself away. His father would go mad if he knew, though.

So, why tell him?

* * *

The next evening, Deirdre was at the Westbury a few minutes before nine.

'But I can't stay,' she said, apologetically. 'I really can't.'

'By tomorrow I shall really be a man,' Jonathan told her. 'Tomorrow night, same place, same time, stay longer?'

'I'll try,' she promised.

She was intrigued by him but a long way from sure of herself, over him or about anything. There was a kind of armed peace between herself and her father. Anthea hadn't been at the house all day, and had not been mentioned. But although her father was nearer his old self than he had been for months, there was still restraint, and she did not think anything had really changed.

If she did have another clash, then Cliff might be the answer.

Cliff and forgetfulness...

She thought once or twice about John Mannering but did not feel tempted to go and see him again. She saw an exhibition of Lorna Mannering's portraits in a small gallery in the Burlington Arcade and some excellent press notices of it, but the Mannerings and Quinns seemed a thousand miles away; she could hardly imagine how she had screwed up her nerve to plan and to do what she had.

Quinns still attracted her like a magnet; she had to fight the temptation to go there and as the time passed she associated her own mood and the change in her father and his forthcoming marriage with the jewels which were buried beneath the shop.

* * *

Mannering had not felt so satisfied with life for so long that he could not remember.

Once the decisions had been made, he had no second thoughts, was more than ever sure that the new plans were right. Bristow hadn't looked back. Old Josh Larraby confirmed what he had told Bristow and positively refused to be driven down to his sister's home; he enjoyed the journey by train, he said, and wanted to travel at his own pace.

Mannering drove him to Paddington Station and handed his one battered suitcase into the compartment after him, and drove back to Quinns'.

Bristow proposed to move in next week, but would stay here at nights meanwhile; only this week-end was left without someone there by day.

When Mannering entered the shop he sensed a measure of excitement, saw Alec Quartermain with two elderly people, left him to it, and went back to his office. Bristow was on the telephone. Mannering went into the office and saw a cable on his desk, turned it round so that he could read it before he sat down, saw that it was in the International Antique Dealers' Code, but Bristow had decoded it and pencilled the message.

It was from Hishinoto, and read:

I am very glad to inform you all authorities including the Emperor welcome your readiness to cooperate with the Jimmu Tenno Treasures Stop I shall bring them myself three weeks from today and they may remain in your strong-room for as long as you need for the valuation Stop The Treasures will thereafter be offered to national museums which was my great hope Stop Warm thanks for your readiness to cooperate and felicitations
Hioto Hishinoto

As he finished reading there was a knock at the door and on his 'Come in' Bristow entered; the new 'young' Bristow. He entered and closed the door, and the aura of excitement and satisfaction was very marked.

'Have we sold all the stock?' asked Mannering, lightly.

'Not quite,' Bristow said, 'but young Alec has pulled off a deal which set my ears tingling. The couple he is with are the Cohns of Toronto — *please* know the Cohns of Toronto,' Bristow pleaded.

'Timber,' Mannering responded.

'Yes, John, the timber Cohns! They're coming to England to retire and have bought a house in Hanover Terrace which hasn't a stick of furniture in it. Alec was at Oxford with their son, and they came to him for advice. His advice was to allow you to furnish the house for them, John, through Quinns. All they ask is that nothing be less than a hundred years old!' Bristow allowed Mannering time to recover from the shock of that and added more quietly, 'Money is literally no object. If it's all right with you I'd let Alec recommend pieces and styles and you approve before submitting them to the Cohns, who are the most charming couple. If you could spare a few moments . . .'

Mannering went into the shop.

The Cohns were in their sixties, quiet voiced, quietly dressed, more aware of what they wanted than Mannering had expected; and Quartermain, whose commission on this order would not be less than five thousand pounds, had just the right manner of authority and respect with them.

'Mrs. Cohn will be buying a number of *objets d'art* as well as some personal jewellery,' he said to Mannering. 'I promised to ask you if these could be kept in the strong-room here, sir, until their house is ready.'

'Of course,' Mannering said. 'We'll be happy to keep them.'

Nothing could have been more normal than that.

* * *

'John,' Bristow said when Mannering had explained Hishinoto's cable to him, 'you will soon want an extension to that strong-room. When the Cohns' things are here and these things from Japan there won't be a square inch of space left.'

'There isn't much now,' Mannering said.

'Is there any you could store anywhere else?' asked Bristow.

'Nothing of any size,' replied Mannering. 'We could move some of Quinns' things to a safe deposit but I'd rather avoid it if we can. The Jimmu Tenno Treasures won't be here too long, and we'll see how things go. You haven't heard if that couple in the red Mini has been about again, have you?'

'Not as such,' Bristow replied. 'But I had a call from Savile Row Police Station. That young copper who told me about them has been harassed by an accident case he witnessed, and been working all hours. He was on nights last night.'

'Yes?' Mannering asked sharply.

'He thought he saw the younger man of the two men in the Mini. He was with a girl in New Bond Street,' went on Bristow. 'So the copper is keeping his eyes open. Of course it may just be a man who lives near here, or comes here regularly to see what women he can pick up from the local hotels.'

Mannering nodded, and said slowly, 'Yes, of course.'

'Have you heard anything more from Ballantine?' asked Bristow.

'So far, not a word,' Mannering said.

'I can tell you the daughter's back at the Breckon Square house,' said Bristow. 'Hampstead were asked to keep an eye on her, and they checked with West London. That may have proved a storm in a tea cup after all.'

14

Ultimatum

'DEE,' SAID BALLANTINE very quietly to his daughter, 'you should know perfectly well that I can't let you dictate to me about my life. It simply isn't possible.'

They were in his study, overlooking the trees in Breckon Square. The beech were just bursting their buds, and on the well-kept lawn children were playing. At one time Deirdre had played there, sometimes with her mother, sometimes in charge of a nurse. She had been such a long-legged child and Ballantine had spent more time than she or any of the others realised watching her from this window. She was still long-legged but much more shapely, and if he had a regret, it was that their years of closeness might have discouraged her from getting married; might have discouraged her from any normal girl-youth relationship.

'No,' she said, tautly. 'I know it isn't. And I know I've behaved very badly.'

'You've been upset . . .' he began.

'Daddy,' she said, 'there's no need to make excuses for me. I behaved shamefully and but for John Mannering might be in very serious trouble. There was no excuse for it, and I'm sorry. I'm sorry I can't live here if you marry Anthea, too — but I simply can't.'

'I think you've proved that,' her father conceded. 'And

I'm not going to break with Anthea. We are going to get married.'

'That's absolutely final, is it?'

'Yes, Dee, it's absolutely final.'

'I hope you're happy,' Deirdre said with a catch in her breath. 'I hope you're very happy, Daddy. I'll get a small flat somewhere in London, and I may travel a great deal, I've always wanted to.'

'You must do what you think best for yourself.' He sounded much more dispassionate than he felt.

'Yes,' she replied. 'I'm glad I'm comfortably off on my own. I do hope you're happy. I really do.'

She turned, and walked away, her skirt short enough to show how long her legs were with their nice calves and the smooth bend at the knees. He did not move after her, for he knew she was keeping her composure only with a great effort and he did not want to make things worse for her. He went back to the study and left his door ajar but she did not return. He heard the front door close, perhaps twenty minutes later, and stood up to watch her walk towards Knightsbridge. She turned the corner, clear in the light of a street lamp. He did not move for a long time. The temptation to call Anthea was almost overwhelming but somehow he resisted it.

He wondered if Deirdre were going off with the man who had brought her here the other night.

She walked very quickly in fact, not wanting to take a taxi, towards Hyde Park and then through it towards Park Lane and eventually by the side roads she knew so well, to the Westbury. She wondered if Cliff would be there. It would be a strange twist if he were not, after all, but it didn't really matter. It was half past eight, early for their rendezvous, and she could not resist the temptation to go and see Quinns. Possibly Cliff would be there too.

He wasn't; but a young policeman was.

She walked back to the Westbury and waited in the

foyer, having no desire at all to drink alone. It was far too early to assume that he wasn't coming, of course, but she was in a mood to take a gloomy view of any situation.

Suddenly, he appeared.

He moved with complete ease tonight, lean and lithe and clean-cut, and his face lit up at the sight of her. He came across and held out both hands and drew her to her feet. For the first time, he kissed her; and for the first time she felt the firmness of his body.

'My, am I glad you've come!'

'I was rather hoping you would,' she said with the lightness of tone which she found easy when talking to him.

'Had dinner?'

'Yes,' she said.

'Pity,' he retorted. 'There's a nice little place at Wimbledon where we can dine and dance, and another at Richmond, not far away. Will you come and see what they're like, anyhow? We could have supper, and dance a little, and . . .'

He broke off.

She didn't remark on the 'and' but went out with him, to his car which was parked in the other direction this time. He put an arm about her waist but did not allow his hand to stray too far, and when they were in the car, he said in a rather husky voice,

'Dee, I was in a real dither in case you didn't turn up tonight.'

'Were you?' she asked, softly.

'I — I simply can't get you out of my mind.'

'That's very flattering.'

'Flattering! It . . .' he broke off, and turned to look at her. In the reflected light from street lamps and a shop window he looked handsome and virile, and her heart began to beat fast. 'Dee,' he went on. 'I'm not one for fun and games, so to speak, in the back of a car. That's no compliment, and it's not really fun. But I'd be a bloody liar if I didn't tell you that I want to make love to you.'

She said, 'You mean, prove you're a real man.'

'That's it,' he agreed, chokily. 'I — I have a pleasant little place at Wimbledon. I'd love to take you there. I don't really want to sit around or dance and pretend that's everything. I — I think I'd rather break the thing off now than that. But I know some girls even today don't feel the permissive society is really for them. Is it, for you?'

She said, very quietly, 'It doesn't have to be, but it can be.'

'Dee,' he said, 'if you'd prefer it, let me take you home now. Or drop you. Or anything you prefer. But if we go to Wimbledon...'

'Take me to Wimbledon,' she decided, and her voice was almost gay.

* * *

'Dee,' Jonathan said, 'you are — superb.'

'Cliff,' she said, 'humour me.'

'Anything, sweeheart!'

'I don't like talking — afterwards.'

'Oh, I'm sorry!' He leaned over her, as massive as she had half-expected, and kissed her forehead; and as a gesture of understanding he drew the sheet up over her to her shoulders. 'Can you stay for the night?'

'Yes.'

'The week-end?' His voice rose.

'If you don't want to throw me out,' she said lightly.

'Throw *you* out? It would be like throwing away diamonds!'

The picturesque phrase caught at her heart, and she could not hide the fact, and he was quick, surprisingly perceptive with change of mood or expression. How could he know what had happened, that in a way she *had* thrown away diamonds and rubies beyond price. She closed her eyes, and felt a stirring of movement before his lips brushed her eyelids.

'I'm sorry,' he said softly.

'It wasn't remotely your fault.'

'But I hurt you.'

'Circumstances hurt me.'

'Would you like to talk about them?' He could be so gentle and she sensed he could also be so understanding, but she did not want to try to explain and was not sure that even if she tried, that she could.

So she opened her eyes a little and said: 'No. No, please.'

'I won't try to make you. But I hate to see you hurt.'

'It won't, and it won't last,' she lied to him.

He thought with a curious kind of exultation that he now understood what troubled her. She had broken off an engagement! He had not dreamt that he would be so near the spot when he had said 'it would be like throwing away diamonds' but engagement rings were nearly always diamonds, and that was the answer. He had met her when she had been hurt by her fiancé and it didn't greatly matter who had left whom; what mattered was that she was so vulnerable, so ready for the plucking.

And she was a marvel; an absolute winner.

No wonder she was at a loose end for the week-end; she might be even for a longer period, and — my God, she was lovely. Lying like that, she was lovely.

He touched her.

She opened her eyes.

He drew her close.

* * *

He went to sleep before she did; fully satisfied and happy.

She was not in bed when he woke when it was broad daylight and he felt a flare of alarm, but suddenly heard the shower running, and instead of leaping out of bed he lay on his back and smiled at the ceiling. He did not have to go to work that morning and had the whole week-end free!

His telephone bell rang.

'Hallo,' he answered cautiously.

'Hallo, son,' said his father. 'Is all proceeding according to plan?'

'It's perfect!' enthused Jonathan.

'Good,' said his father, with a laugh in his voice. 'You don't happen to know who she is yet, do you?'

'I know she's just had an engagement broken — could be a marriage I suppose! — and I have her on the re-bound, as it were.'

'Couldn't be better,' declared David Cleff. 'I'll call you later, Clifford.'

He rang off.

A few minutes afterwards Deirdre whom he knew only as Dee came in, wrapped in one of his summer weight dressing-gowns, pale blue and white in colour. Her hair was piled high on the top of her head, her face was shiny and rosy, like her forehead. He hitched himself up on the pillows and beckoned and she came across and sat on the bed with her legs under her. Although she was so near he had a sense of aloofness; perhaps it was only diffidence, or a shyness brought on by the daylight.

'I wish my dressing-gown could make me look half as good as it makes you look,' he said lightly.

'Perhaps it would if you wore it,' she said, and he chuckled. 'Clifford, am I dreaming or did you invite me to stay for the week-end?'

'I invited you.'

'Did I accept?' she asked.

'And you weren't drunk,' he assured her.

'There was something the matter with me! I've no

clothes, no night things, nothing except what I had on my back or in my handbag. I — I left in a hurry last night and I didn't really know what I was doing.'

'Dee,' he said, soberly. 'I had the strongest impression that you knew exactly what you were doing.'

She stared; then coloured slightly, and laughed partly to cover her confusion.

'I mean when I stormed out of my house.'

'Oh.'

'I really haven't a thing, and — well, I don't want to go back for anything this morning.'

'Then don't.'

'You don't happen to have a spare toothbrush, do you?'

'No, but I know where I can buy you one,' he said, then hesitated, sat upright and slid his hands inside her gown to her shoulders, which felt cool and very soft. 'Dee — you didn't walk out on your husband last night, did you?'

She looked astounded. 'Gracious, no!'

'Thank heavens for that,' he said. 'I have a terror of vengeful husbands! Er — you stay here as long as you like. I really mean that. This house belongs to my father, he lives downstairs and I live up here. It works out very well, we're not in each other's pockets but we are in close touch. I'm out during the week, of course, and he is some of the time.' Seeking an explanation for his father, he went on almost too hurriedly, 'He's in insurance. Will you stay?'

'May I for a few days?'

'It will be glorious! Mind you, there are certain things you'll have to do in return, such as cook breakfast, make my morning tea, do all the things a wife is expected to do for her husband. I — '

Suddenly, his hands moved.

* * *

'I can't be in love with him, can I?' Deirdre asked herself, when he had gone out to buy some odds and ends.

* * *

'I can't be falling in love with her, can I?' Jonathan Cleff asked himself as he drove round to the shops. 'I haven't felt like this for — oh, a hell of a long time.'

When he came back he found his father at the street door, and David Cleff simply insisted. 'Find out who she is, Jonathan. I must know.'

'Anyone would think you thought she was a spy,' Jonathan complained sharply.

'Stranger things have happened,' his father replied. 'Just find out.'

* * *

'Cliff,' Deirdre said, later in the morning. 'I don't want to tell you who I am, yet. I am not a married woman. I have had a quarrel with my family and left home so that I could forget things for a while. I would love to stay here for a few days but if you must ask a lot of questions I shall leave and go to a hotel. Please don't make me do that.'

'All right,' Jonathan said at once. 'That's a deal, and I'm sorry I pushed.' But for the first time since he had brought her here he began to wonder whether there was any justification for his father's suspicions, and he was quite determined to find out who she was. One thing was certain: families with houses in Breckon Square, S.W.1. were invariably very wealthy.

Now and again he was teased by the thought that he had seen her before somewhere but simply couldn't remember where.

15

Fears

'JOHN,' LORNA SAID, 'you're worried, aren't you?'

'Against my better judgment—yes,' Mannering answered from his big chair in the study.

'Is there any specific reason?' Lorna was sitting on the pouffe.

'Yes and no,' he vacillated.

'Is it about the Jimmu Tenno Treasures? They're due here next week, aren't they?'

It was already two weeks since the Japanese had sent the cable, and since the excitement over Deirdre Ballantine. They had been uneventful and yet for them, both busy weeks, and this was one of the occasions when they had been able to relax and talk.

'Partly the Jimmus,' Mannering admitted. 'Partly because . . .' he broke off, ruefully. 'I think I'm worried about me!'

'Go on like this and I shall be too,' Lorna retorted. 'I would have thought . . .' she broke off.

'Don't pull your punches,' he urged.

'I would have thought you'd had the most successful year you've ever known.'

'So would I,' agreed Mannering. 'In fact I'm sure that's true.'

'And with Bristow there instead of Larraby, and with

Alec Quartermain doing so well, what more can you want? Lorna asked. She spoke lightly, without any hint of reproach or complaint: rather she was puzzled and looking for a way to help.

'I know,' he said. 'Nothing. I don't think I do want anything. I'm just not easy in my mind.'

'Is there going to be too much in the strong-room?'

'A few weeks ago I wouldn't have thought so,' Mannering answered. 'Bill and I have spent a lot of time shifting the things around to make room for the Jimmus in the two end chambers, and we're sending some things to a strong-room in a nearby bank. The actual handling of so much might be the explanation, of course.' He sat up in his chair and rested a hand lightly on her shoulder. 'I shall get over it.'

'Darling,' she said, 'you won't hide any dangers from me, will you?'

Thoughtfully and with some deliberation he answered, 'No, my love, but nor will I talk too much about vague worries and uncertainties and moods and fancies.'

'I don't see why not,' Lorna argued. 'If you don't talk about them with me, who are you going to talk with them about?'

'Perhaps with myself!'

'You *are* keeping something back,' she said, mildly accusing.

'Not consciously,' he assured her.

She pressed his hand and then stood up and went to the settle, which had been unlocked earlier and he would lock again before leaving the study. He watched her, his heart beating fast. She lifted out some jewel-cases and a small jewelled sword as well as a wash-leather bag which held uncut diamonds, then pressed a tiny protuberance at the side of the settle. There was a sharp click of sound. She saw a false bottom move back, and after a moment leaned further inside and brought out a large, leather-bound book.

She put this on the floor and brought out two more, then closed the settle.

Mannering got up and picked up the books, and carried them to the pouffe, opened one and stood the other two alongside. His own photograph stared out at him, but he looked much younger. He opened another book, and on the second page the headline of an old newspaper screamed:

The Baron Strikes Again.

Last night, in the heart of Mayfair, the jewel thief extraordinary known as the Baron broke into the home of Lord Tolbemayer and stole the Tolbemayer collection of precious stones — valued at over one million pounds. The daring thief gained entry to the house by the roof.

Chief Inspector William Bristow, in charge of the investigation, described the raid as one of the most brilliant and daring of his experience. 'At any moment,' he told a *Globe* reporter, 'the criminal could have slipped and broken his neck.'

Several other press cuttings describing the same robbery were in the book, and on the last page of the entries a smaller cutting which said:

Anonymous Gift of £250,000

The management of the East London Dockers' Children's Club were stunned yesterday by an anonymous gift of a quarter of a million pounds, the largest in the club's history. New club premises enabling facilities to be provided for at least another two hundred orphans are now assured...

These were some of many reports, all vividly written; but gradually their mood changed. In the early days they were all about the Baron, jewel thief extraordinary who robbed the rich to help the poor, but as the years passed there were more and more references to John Mannering of Quinns. He might be consulted by the police after the loss of a famous collection of jewels, or acting as a private detective to help some individual in need. There was no positive association between the Baron and Mannering but it was obviously implied.

There were references in the early reports to Mannering and Lorna: their engagement, her painting, some violent attacks on them in this very flat! In the last of the three books there were references to big sales at Quinns, several to attempted thefts at Quinns, to big purchases which Mannering had made for clients at some of the major auctions in London and other capital cities. But mostly the theme was crime and, increasingly, the fight against crime.

As they turned the pages, Mannering leaning forward in his chair and Lorna sitting cross-legged by his side, they seemed to be reliving their own past.

At last, she stopped turning, and looked up at him.

'You miss the excitement so much, darling.'

'It *can't* be as simple as that,' he replied, almost angrily.

'I think it is, though. If instead of Deirdre Ballantine coming here and taking the jewels and you going straight off and getting them back, you were still looking for them ...' she broke off.

'You think I'd be so busy worrying and chasing after them that I wouldn't have time to brood?'

'Yes,' Lorna answered, quite seriously.

'Could be, I suppose,' he mused, 'and I confess I'd like to hear from Ballantine or Anthea Ross or the girl. But I don't think you're right.'

'You're not hankering after the old excitements?'

His eyes glistened. 'Oh, I'd still enjoy them! But I don't think they're my main worry, darling, romantic though that would be. No: I'm simply uneasy. I've a sense that something's out of hand, and it may simply be that Quinns *is* too big.' When she didn't answer, he went on: 'Too big for me to handle and therefore too big in spite of all the help there is. Do you think I'm crazy?'

'Not necessarily,' Lorna replied.

He pretended to tweak her ear, actually leaned forward to kiss her forehead, and as he did so the telephone bell rang. It was after ten o'clock, not really late but unexpected. Lorna shifted her position so that Mannering could reach the telephone from where he sat. As he picked it up her expression was positively wicked, and she mouthed,

'The police desperately need your help!'

'Or Mrs. Culbertson's been robbed,' he breathed, and put the receiver to his ear, announcing, 'This is John Mannering.'

'John,' a man said, and he recognised Lucas Ballantine on the instant. 'I know it's late but I'm so deeply worried. I wonder if I could come round and see you?'

'Of course,' Mannering answered, and asked quietly, 'Is it Deirdre?'

'Yes,' said Ballantine. 'She's vanished, and I've neither seen nor heard of her for two weeks. To make it worse, Anthea blames herself for Deirdre's disappearance, I blame myself, and — well, we both feel desperately anxious to see her again. Her absence is a constant, corroding anxiety, and yet I don't want to go to the police again. I asked them to drop watching for her when she came home, and — well, the truth is that I want to persuade you to look for her again.'

* * *

David Cleff said in a hard voice: 'Where do you say you met her?'

'At the Westbury.'

'What the hell were you doing at the Westbury?'

'I was having a drink, I can have a drink where I want too, can't I?'

'You're lying to me,' David said, and his expression made his face look ugly. 'You were outside Quinns.'

'I wasn't! I...'

'You can't keep away from the place, you bloody fool!'

'Don't talk to me like that,' blustered Jonathan. 'I'm in this as much as you are.'

'You could wreck the whole plan!'

'Listen, I haven't been near Hart Row for weeks I tell you. Okay, I went to the Westbury the day after we'd decided to go ahead, so what was wrong with that? And okay, I went for a walk, but there's no law against that. I saw Dee and she looked my kind so I followed her. Is it a crime to follow a girl, even if you do want to lay her?'

'Were you looking into Quinns?' his father demanded roughly.

'I've told you — no!'

'But you were in Hart Row.'

'*She* was in Hart Row, I just followed her.'

'Breaking your neck to look in at Quinns, I bet you.'

'I wasn't! And I haven't been there since, *I'm* not a fool.'

'Sometimes I wonder.'

'You've a bloody nerve, talking to me like that,' protested Jonathan, weakly.

'Son,' said David Cleff, 'we're on to the job of a lifetime. I've told you that I won't have to work any more when this is over, and I've also told you I'll stop at nothing to pull it off. And nothing includes making sure that little tart upstairs can't talk.'

'She doesn't *know* anything!'

'You picked her up in Hart Row. For all you know she works for Mannering.'

'Oh, no, she doesn't,' Jonathan retorted, even more weakly.

'Then who is she? How is it she can lay about upstairs all day? What is she hiding from? Come on, son, it's time you told me the truth. You once told me her name was Deirdre Ball and she'd run away from home, but I want to know her real name.'

Jonathan said, 'It *is* Deirdre ...'

'Deirdre what?'

'Ballantine.'

'Where does she live?'

'I can tell you that, too — she lives at 28 Breckon Square.'

'Are you *sure*?'

'Yes,' Jonathan replied bitterly. 'She's a classy one all right. She quarrelled with her family and I happened to be there to catch her when she fell. And, boy, is she the works!'

David Cleff was saying, 'Ballantine, Ballantine,' to himself, and stretched out for the telephone directory by the telephone which stood next to his chair. 'How do you know that's her real name?'

'It's on her passport — does that satisfy you?'

'It's better,' his father conceded. 'Ball — Ball — Ballantine — Sir Lucas Ballantine of 28 Breckon Square, London, S.W.1.'

'There!' cried Jonathan. 'Does that satisfy you?'

His father was sitting very still. Even Jonathan, angry though he had been, could see that something was the matter, something very serious. He gulped, but did not speak. His father stood up slowly and went to a writing bureau on the other side of the room, unlocked a drawer and took out a manilla folder. Inside this were dozens of photographs of lists which Jonathan had not seen before. Peering over his father's shoulder he saw that the top ones were headed: *Jack Diamond — Insurance*. Beneath the address which was printed below this were two lines which read: *Schedule of Goods Insured on behalf of John*

Mannering, Esq., of Quinns, Hart Row, London, W.1. Beneath this another line which read: *Insuring Company: Several Lloyds underwriters.*

Then followed a list of jewellery described in a way which made Jonathan's eyes glisten; it was almost as if he had forgotten the conflict between himself and his father.

David Cleff said in a grating voice, '*Look.*' And his finger pointed to a line which said: *A Collection of Diamonds and Rubies in seventeen different pieces... the property of Sir Lucas Ballantine, Bt.*

There was utter silence in the room except for Jonathan's heavy breathing; his father seemed to make no sound at all until slowly he moved away from the writing desk, looked at the ceiling, and asked thinly,

'Do you still think it was a coincidence?'

'It—it doesn't mean a thing. Her—her father's got some jewellery at Quinns, that's all.'

'Jonathan,' said David Cleff, very softly, 'I'm going to talk to that girl, and I'm going to scare the wits out of her. If she can't explain what she was doing at Hart Row, then I'm going to choke the life out of her.'

There was a long pause; a tense pause; before Jonathan seemed to throw back his shoulders and move between his father and the door to the hall.

'No, you're not,' he said harshly.

'Yes I am. Nothing's going to stop me from breaking into Quinns.'

'Dad,' Jonathan Cleff said, in a taut voice, 'I'll find out what you want to know.'

'You're like a piece of clay in her hands! I'll see her, and...' David began to go forward.

'Dad,' Jonathan said, 'don't go.'

'Like hell I'm going!'

'Don't try to get past me,' Jonathan said. 'I'll find out if...'

His father swayed to one side, Jonathan went to stop

him, the older man swung in the opposite direction and thrust his son to one side with a hand planted on his chest. Jonathan lost his balance and staggered as his father darted to the door.

'*Don't go up there!*' Jonathan roared.

David pulled open the door and sprang outside—and then stopped and stared towards the staircase. For Deirdre was half way down. She carried her big handbag in her right hand, and clutched the banister rail with her left. She checked her stealthy movement at the sight of David, who seemed to be struck dumb.

Jonathan came from behind him, and heard his heavy breathing.

'Don't you see who she is,' David said. 'She was going into Mannering's when we were sitting in the car outside. She could put a finger on us any time she wanted to. With her around we'd never be safe.'

At last he moved, towards her; and at last she moved, springing down the stairs in what was obviously a desperate effort to reach the street door before he could stop her.

16

Life or Death

DEIRDRE HAD HEARD the two men talking soon after Jonathan had gone out of the room. There was a shaft, either for ventilation or for a tiny lift, in a corner of the small room which had become 'hers', and two or three times before she had heard father and son talking, but it had always been good natured, often banter, and her feeling towards the older man whom she had not seen had been rather pleasant. She had been curiously contented here, reading, listening to records and watching television, going out for walks across Wimbledon Common on her own. In one way it had been exactly the holiday she needed.

In another it troubled her.

To spend a week-end with a man was — well, not abnormal, was in these days quite common. So it was to live with a man. But this was wrong, because she no longer felt that she was falling in love with Cliff, only that she liked him.

Before very long she would have to leave.

It was a part of her life lifted out of the everyday, a period she knew she would look back on as if it were a dream. She did not know what to do next, but she was much calmer in her mind. The truth was that Cliff, like the little apartment, had been a sanctuary.

One thing had puzzled her: Cliff had shown no interest at all in the future. Like her, he seemed content to live for the day. He left each week-day morning at half-past seven and was back each evening at half-past five, when he bathed, changed, and was soon ready to take her out to a meal or to have a simple meal which she prepared; and she always enjoyed preparing it.

She had a feeling that he was waiting for some change of events.

This morning, Saturday, they had lazed for an hour in bed, and it had astonished her that she could feel so 'married'. After a breakfast of bacon and eggs he had gone downstairs 'to have a word with the old man'. By chance, she had gone to the cupboard as the older man had said roughly:

'You could wreck the whole plan.'

Plan, she had thought: what plan?

Gradually, the truth had come to her: the plan was to raid Quinns.

At first she had felt numbed and bewildered that she could have misjudged Cliff so much, but gradually the full implication had come to her. Both men in their different ways were ruthless, and would let nothing get in their way.

She had to leave, quickly. There was grave danger here.

She moved from the cupboard, where a few clothes which she had bought were hanging, put her toilet accessories in the big leather bag, and then tip-toed towards the door. From a state of numbed shock she was reaching a state of quivering nerves. Something in the tone of the older man convinced her that she was in acute danger.

When she went into the living-room she could hear only the rumble of voices and did not know what was being said; but now and again voices were raised, as if they were quarrelling. She reached the door which opened on to the landing, and the voices grew louder but the words were still not distinguishable.

She was halfway down the stairs when a door opened and the older man stepped out. From the room beyond came a roar from Cliff, 'Don't go up there!' and then his father went rigid and Cliff appeared.

After the first shocked moment, Deirdre sprang downwards, for she was nearer the street door than either of the men. But the older one moved with startling speed, not at her but towards the door. He stopped with his back towards it, so that she had no chance of getting past him.

The only hope, the only possible hope, was to attract attention, and she opened her mouth to scream. Only one scream came, before Cliff leapt at her from the side, and a hand which had so often caressed her slapped over her mouth and caused sharp pain. When she tried to bite him and struggle he flung his free arm round her shoulders with a force which seemed to crush her flesh into her bones. Almost in the same movement he picked her up cradling her in his arms, and carried her upstairs; and it hurt so much she did not kick or struggle. He pushed the flat door open with his knee, carried her through the living-room and his bedroom, into the room which had become hers.

He dropped her on to the bed.

She was terrified by the expression on his face; it was as if the man who had been so gentle as her lover had suddenly become a beast.

Over his shoulder was his father. At that angle the likeness between them was uncanny; both were breathing harshly, both had their mouths open, both had their teeth bared. But she was more afraid of Cliff than of his father; it was as if a great revulsion of feeling had swept over him, carrying him in one gigantic swoop from love to hate. He stood close to her small bed, bending over her, his hands crooked only two feet away from her throat.

'Son,' his father said. 'She has to talk.'

Cliff didn't speak or move.

'Move aside,' his father said. 'I'll make her.'

Cliff didn't move but he began to speak in a low-pitched, growling voice which seemed to come with an effort.

'Did anyone send you, you bitch? Come on, tell me. Did anyone send you?'

She managed to stammer, 'N-no one s-sent me. I—I t-t-told you the truth.'

'You were spying on me!'

'No,' she said, gasping. 'Oh, God, no.'

'You lying bitch, you made a fool of me!' His hands moved closer to her throat, the fingers tensing and untensing as if they were made of steel coil. His teeth were so white, his expression so cruel.

'No,' she said. 'I told you the truth.'

'You were spying...'

'Until—until I heard you talking just now, I'd no idea what you planned to do.'

'You're lying!' he cried.

'Jonathan,' interrupted his father, 'let me talk to her.'

'She'll lie to you just as she lied to me. Why, before I'll let any woman make a fool out of me...'

'Did you know your father had some jewels at Quinns?' David Cleff asked.

'*Know?*' she gasped. 'Of course I knew!'

'So you did know...' began Jonathan whom she knew as Clifford, but there was less venom in his voice and he allowed his father to push him a little to one side.

'Had you seen us before?' David asked.

'I've told you,' she said. 'I've told you. No.'

'Why did you go to Hart Row the night my son was there?' asked David.

'That's right—explain that if you can,' Jonathan *alias* Clifford said hoarsely, but his anger had evaporated, and she thought he was frightened now. She knew that of these two the father was much the stronger character, for under sudden pressure the son had simply gone to pieces. He had backed away and was leaning against a tiny chest of drawers.

'I don't know whether you'll even begin to understand,' she replied. 'But my father is going to remarry and that means some of the family jewellery will belong to his new wife while she's alive, and not to me. I — I hated the thought of that, and I knew the jewellery was at Quinns. I kept going there, somehow I couldn't keep away.'

Her words fell off into silence.

She could not be sure but thought the others believed her; thought the change of expressions was the passing from suspicion to acceptance of her story and for a moment or two her heart felt lighter. She did not tell them about what she had done, how she had stolen the jewellery because it seemed to her that no one could possibly believe that.

Suddenly, Clifford *alias* Jonathan exclaimed, 'So you weren't spying on me.'

'Of course I wasn't,' she said, a note of asperity in her voice.

'There you are,' Jonathan turned in triumph to his father. 'She *wasn't* spying on me. I was quite right to trust her.'

Slowly, David Cleff said, 'Yes, you were, weren't you?'

'I — I was so tired of the family quarrels I just had to get away,' Deirdre said. 'You were a godsend, Cliff. I don't know what I would have done without you.'

'That's all right, baby! No harm done and no hard feelings, I hope.'

She looked at him with an expression empty of the disgust she was beginning to feel, and she made herself say, 'Of course not.' He was not the one to be nervous of, however, not now. She could not understand the expression on the older man's face but it frightened her, in a different way, at least as much as Clifford had when she had thought he was going to put his fingers round her throat, and strangle her.

David asked very quietly, 'How much did you hear?'

'I — I don't understand you.'

'How much did you hear me and Jonathan — Cliff — saying?'

'Not — not very much,' she said. 'I — I heard you shouting and that scared me. I don't know . . .'

He startled them both by swinging round towards the cupboard and opening the door, looking at the far wall, and then speaking clearly. 'Has this been blocked up, I wonder?' His voice did not echo. He moved away, turned to his son, and said in the same clear voice, 'Go down to my flat, Jonathan, and talk in a normal tone of voice.' When Jonathan looked puzzled, he went on, 'There was a time when you could hear every word from my front room if you had that door open.' As Jonathan began to move towards the landing as if he still did not fully understand, David asked Deirdre sharply, 'Did you hear everything we said today?'

She knew, now, that it would be useless to lie; and so she said, 'Yes, I did.'

'You know we are going to raid Quinns?'

She gulped, then replied, 'Yes.'

David said, 'Okay, son, you needn't go downstairs, we know what we want to know.' He looked down at Deirdre, and she hated the expression in his eyes, because it told her what was passing through his mind. Slowly, he shook his head, and slowly he said, 'That's a pity.'

'Pity,' echoed Jonathan.

She said, 'I — I won't tell anyone.'

'If you got out of here the first thing you would do would be to telephone your father, or Mannering, or the police,' stated David Cleff as if with absolute assurance. 'You couldn't get to a telephone quick enough.'

She made herself mutter, 'No. No, I swear . . .'

'Swearing on the altar at St. Paul's or St. Peter's wouldn't make any difference,' David said, heavily. 'We couldn't trust you out of our sight.'

Jonathan didn't speak.

Deirdre wished she could shrink away from the older man, could escape from the full significance of what he was saying, but there was no escape. *She knew what these two planned to do.* They could not possibly release her before or after carrying out the planned raid. They would never be safe from her for as long as she was alive. The expression in David's eyes was really the passing of the sentence of death.

'I — I'll watch her,' Jonathan said.

Inwardly she shivered.

'Son, watching isn't going to be quite good enough.' David turned his gaze towards his son, and Deirdre's inward shiver grew worse; she had never seen anything more calculating in a man. 'We have to lock the little lady up.'

She gasped, 'No!'

'Oh, but we are,' insisted David Cleff. 'We'll shut you in this room, and lock the door and window. One of us will come and let you out every two or three hours. But don't try to attract attention, don't break the window. Just one try will be your last act. You do understand, don't you?'

She nodded, mutely.

'Jonathan,' the older man said. 'Dee will need some food and drink, you'd better go and get some.' He waited for his son to leave and Jonathan went slowly, as if he did not really understand what had happened, or how completely his father had taken control.

When he was alone with Deirdre, David went on in a cold voice, 'My son is sometimes sentimental, I never am.'

She could believe him.

'One shout; one attempt to escape; and I'll kill you with my own hands,' he said. He crossed to the side of the bed and picked up the bag, tipping it upside down so that all the contents fell out. Among them was a small sewing kit which included a pair of scissors. 'You won't need these,' he declared, and put them in his pocket. 'Jonathan will get you plenty of books and you can have a radio.'

She actually said, 'Thank you.'

He stared down at her, then turned away.

* * *

There was only one reason why David Cleff did not kill the girl now; if he did, Jonathan's nerve would almost certainly go to pieces. He himself wasn't quite ready for the raid on Quinns or he would have staged it this week-end. He had the passports, the letters of confirmation from overseas banks, everything he needed except some reasonably safe-to-use explosive, an improvement on nitroglycerine, with which to blow the safes in the strong-room.

When they had the jewels, when all the loot was theirs, Jonathan wouldn't give a damn about what happened to Deirdre. He knew Jonathan.

* * *

'I won't let him hurt you,' Jonathan whom she had known as Clifford said in a whisper. 'Don't worry, I won't let him hurt you.'

She took the coffee which he had brought up, not dreaming that it was drugged; but within five minutes she was trying to fight off drowsiness, and within ten she was dead to the world.

* * *

None of Bristow's friends at the Yard had any information about Deirdre Ballantine this time. The only report which had reached Bristow and about which he had told Mannering that Saturday morning, was that she had been seen by the zealous policeman in Hart Row over two weeks ago; and the same policeman had noticed that for two nights running the same red Morris had been parked near the Westbury Hotel after the hours of restriction. He had noticed the registration number YXL 1243 and jotted it down in his report.

'If this were an official inquiry the police would have had the car traced,' Bristow said, 'but I can't expect them to trace it just as a favour to me. If Ballantine would report his daughter as officially missing I could do something.'

'From what he told me, the police wouldn't regard her as missing,' Mannering said. 'She left deliberately, she is old enough to know her own mind, and she took her passport. They'd argue that she may be out of the country. How many of your police friends will keep an eye open for the red Mini?'

'A few dozen,' Bristow said.

'We need a lot more. We need . . .' Mannering broke off suddenly, as a new thought entered his head, and Bristow watched with a mixture of admiration and exasperation as he checked a number in his diary and immediately dialled. Almost at once a woman answered with a deep pleasant voice.

'This is Mrs. Anthea Ross.'

'Mrs. Ross,' Mannering said, 'this is John Mannering, and I've just thought of a way in which you might be able to help find Deirdre.'

'I will try anyway at all,' Anthea said with quiet emphasis.

'You work a great deal among the Jamaican and Pakistani immigrant groups, don't you?' Mannering said.

'I most certainly do,' Anthea Ross answered.

'It might help — I'm far from sure but it might help if I could trace a red Morris Mini, with the registration number YXL 1243,' Mannering told her. 'If you could ask your friends — particularly in the religious and social groups this week-end, or . . .'

'I can arrange for twenty or thirty thousand people to be looking out for the car,' Anthea assured him, and there was warmth and feeling in her voice. 'I will start at once.' She rang off before Mannering could speak again.

17

The Jimmu Tenno Treasures

'TWO BIRDS WITH one stone,' Bristow remarked as Mannering put down the receiver. 'Why don't I have some bright ideas like that?' He was obviously very pleased, not only because of the effort which would be made but because it cleared the decks for what he felt was their greatest problem: the security of the Jimmu Tenno treasures. 'We should have Hishinoto's cable giving us the flight number any time now, John. Are you going to be at the airport to meet it?'

'No,' Mannering said. 'Anyone who noticed me would know there was a special reason. Have you alerted the Airport Police?'

'Of course.'

'And the Yard?'

'The cargo will be moved from the aircraft by the regular staff,' Bristow told him. 'As Hishinoto has brought shipments in by air before no one is going to be surprised when two Japanese hold a watching brief. The Jimmu Tenno treasures are in a specially marked consignment of lightweight steel cases, and will be loaded into the same plain van. The van will be led by me in my own car and a police Y-car which no one will recognise and followed by Hishinoto in a private hire car and a second police vehicle. *There's* influence for you!'

'It sounds exactly right,' Mannering said.

'As you outlined it and I've only laid it on, I hope it is,' Bristow rejoined. 'I have arranged for two policemen to be on duty at Quinns and two plainclothes detectives, as well as Alec Quartermain. Another of Hishinoto's staff will be there, too.'

Mannering nodded.

'There's one thing we haven't decided,' he said.

'What's that?'

'Whether to take the shipment in by the front door in Hart Row or at the back?'

'Hart Row, I think,' Mannering replied, 'and I'll be there to receive it.'

'Within half an hour of getting the cases to Hart Row everything should be safely in the strong-room,' Bristow said, checking a list of his plans. 'I think that's the lot, John — or is there something I've forgotten?' he asked suspiciously, seeing Mannering smile faintly.

'Alec, you and I are the only three to go down into the strong-room,' Mannering remarked.

'Ah. Yes.'

'Will the special precautions be maintained until we've taken everything downstairs?'

'Yes,' said Bristow, and went on thoughtfully, 'John, it doesn't cost us much to have this special police protection. Shall we keep it going all the week-end?'

'No,' Mannering answered without hesitation. 'I just want to be sure there's no trouble while the treasure is actually being moved. When it's in the strong-room it's safe.' He turned Bristow's list so that he could read it, checked each item on the schedule, laughed at himself, and said *sotto voce*, 'I suppose Hishinoto made me feel the treasure could be full of ghosts or laden with curses! I'll be glad when everything's here.'

As he finished the telephone bell rang, and he picked up the receiver briskly. Immediately he nodded to Bristow, who picked up a pencil and wrote down exactly what Mannering repeated into the telephone.

'A cable from Tokyo. Pan Am Flight 1 from Tokyo was due to leave airport at 18.30 last night and will arrive at London Heath Row at 17.05 today. The cable is signed Hishinoto . . . Will you repeat that, please? . . .' He listened to the repeat, said 'thank you', put down the receiver and said with relief, 'Now we won't be long. It will take you an hour to reach the airport. You'd better have a snack before you leave.'

'I shall have one there, while I'm talking to the airport police,' Bristow said. 'You need some lunch, John.'

'I'll get some,' Mannering promised. 'In fact I'll come with you as far as your car.'

Bristow opened the front door of Quinns, which had its self-locking device, and they walked towards Hart House, where Bristow's car as well as Mannering's was parked in the carriage way, for the underground garages were not used at week-ends. Bristow drove off in his black Rover, and Mannering walked through an alley which led to a series of Mayfair streets and to a pub where he could get some cold chicken, a Scotch egg and some coffee. The meat round the egg was soft and appetising, and he felt well-fed when he retraced his steps.

In the entrance to the garage ramp was a truck with the name of a construction company on it. One man was getting down from the cab of the truck, another was bending over a crack in the surface of the ramp. Although he noticed them Mannering did not give the men a second thought; some kind of repairs were being done at the week-end, which was the usual time; and work on these office blocks never seemed to end.

* * *

'That was Mannering!' exclaimed Jonathan Cleff.

'I'm glad you're keeping your eyes open,' his father retorted.

'But if he's here at week-ends . . .'

'Son,' interrupted David Cleff, 'he's certain to be here at some week-ends, but that doesn't mean he'll be here next Saturday. If he is, we know what to do. As it is we've done exactly what we wanted to do : made a quick visit, so that no one who is around here on Saturdays will be surprised to see us again. It's all part of the plan. This time next week you'll be working on that drill. The two watchmen will be easy. They meet at ten o'clock on Friday night, and report only if there's an emergency. They won't know there is one! I can lock them up in a store-room, a couple of days in cold storage won't do them any harm. The truck will be parked so that no one can see where you're drilling. It's as good as done,' he went on, gripping Jonathan's arm. 'Mannering didn't look at us twice, and you saw where he parks his car.'

Jonathan replied in a rough voice, 'Okay. So it's okay.'

'We needn't stay long today,' his father said.

In fact he had come because Jonathan had been so edgy after the trouble with the girl. It would have been impossible to stay around the house in Wimbledon all day, letting him brood. The best thing now, David decided, was to park the van at a parking place not far from a big construction job where they had left the red Morris Mini, go back to the house, let the boy spend half an hour with the girl, and then go out and play some golf.

He wished he could choke the life out of the girl now. She was a constant anxiety, if not a constant threat. She did not know they had gone out, of course, but there was always a chance that she would come round before they got back and make some effort to escape.

He need not have worried, for she was still unconscious when they returned.

Jonathan, by his father's side, said uneasily,

'She will be all right, won't she?'

'A good long sleep is just what she needs,' his father assured him. 'And while she's asleep, I'm going to change the glass in that window. If she lost her nerve she could hurt herself breaking the glass that's there now.'

'Where the hell can we get unbreakable glass?' demanded Jonathan.

'At a do-it-yourself shop in Putney,' David said, confidently.

* * *

In fact all he did was to climb a ladder and stick the toughened glass on to the other pane from the outside. This way it could not possibly attract a neighbour's attention, and it made the room virtually soundproof. When it was done, Deirdre was beginning to stir.

'Let's leave her,' he said. 'She'll be in just the right mood for a little company when we get back.'

Jonathan hesitated before turning his back on her, watched his father secure the room door not only with a key but with a bolt he had bought at the same time as the glass. He said nothing. But his mood greatly improved as he went out on to the Merton golf course, and it was one of his days. He was hitting the ball hard and straight down the fairway, while to make his afternoon perfect, his father could do nothing right. When the other suggested dinner together before going back, he agreed without hesitation; it was almost as if he had forgotten Deirdre.

* * *

She had come round.

She knew she had been drugged, but she felt no painful after-effects, only muzziness, and at least she was still alive.

How long would they leave her here alive?

Where were they?

Did she have any chance at all of escaping?

She got off the bed and went to the narrow window, from which there was a view of back gardens and the windows of one or two other houses. Almost at once she saw the double-glazing, and she knew why that had been done. Her heart thumping sickeningly, she went to the door; and she could tell, after pushing it gently, that it was bolted as well as locked.

'Oh, my God!' she breathed. 'They'll never let me go.'

* * *

Meanwhile Flight Number 1 landed at Heathrow as smoothly as nine-hundred and ninety-nine flights out of a hundred, and the familiar safety precautions were relaxed, the fire-tenders went to stand by for other aircraft, only the watchful airport police were particularly interested in the cargo. It was unloaded and taken to Customs where an officer examined it in a privately-marked part of the examination hall, checked all the entries and allowed the treasures to be resealed.

Bristow watched.

The little convoy of cars and van left at four o'clock. By five it turned into Hart Row. No one had followed, no one showed any interest here. One of the policemen on duty was the one who had talked to Mannering three weeks ago, and when the cases were all safely inside Mannering's office — which was as far as any non-member of the staff was allowed to see them — and Hishinoto and his men had gone, Mannering asked him,

'Have you ever wondered what it's like inside Quinns?'

'Yes, sir — always fascinated me.'

'When do you go off duty?'

'I'm off duty now, sir. I have to sign off from the station but that's a formality.' He cast a sidelong glance at Bristow as if still very conscious of that man's recent status. 'I could go and sign off and come back, if that would be convenient.'

'Have a look round in half an hour,' suggested Bristow, and he smiled across at Mannering. 'We can get those things unloaded.'

'Keeping me up to my job, are you!' Mannering said lightly.

With young Quartermain they shifted the cases from the office to the strong-room, and it was half an hour almost to the minute when they had finished, and half an hour to the second when the young policeman reappeared.

His name, he told them, was Abbott.

He was utterly fascinated, and when he left a little after six o'clock, he said earnestly,

'It's fabulous, sir — absolutely fabulous. And that's why I keep an eye on anyone who appears to be taking a special interest in Quinns. It would be a sacrilege to break in here, an absolute sacrilege. I hope you didn't think I was being over-officious about the two men in that car a few weeks ago. Funny thing I saw it again a few nights later, wasn't it?'

'Very funny,' agreed Mannering. 'And I was very glad you took such notice. You will let me or Mr. Bristow know if you ever see it again, won't you?'

'Be sure of that, sir — absolutely sure,' Abbott said, and when he had gone Bristow remarked with a crooked grin,

'If he goes on like that he'll be known as 'Absolute' Abbott before long! I know one thing for sure: if he ever sees YXL 1243 again he'll be round here like a bullet from a gun!'

But 'Absolute' Abbott did not see it that week-end.

Nor did any of the thousands of people who were on the alert for it, although at least a dozen of them passed it during the next forty-eight hours. Because it rained;

from early evening on the Saturday and through all of Sunday there was a steady downpour, and only those who really had to go out left their homes. David Cleff, desperately anxious to keep his son's mind occupied, let him sit with Deirdre in his own room watching television on the Saturday evening, after a meal which he himself prepared. He was far from sure how Jonathan felt about his 'Dee' but was positive that he had to handle the situation very carefully. After a fashion, Jonathan was 'in love' but his behaviour when he had suspected that the girl had spied on him was an indication of how brittle that 'love' was.

If he, David, could prove that she was a threat, Jonathan would probably deal with her without compunction.

'No,' David told himself, dispassionately. 'If she's killed his nerve might crack. We've got to keep her alive until next Saturday. When we've got the stuff it won't matter a damn.' He repeated this to himself time and time again, as if he desperately needed convincing.

On the Saturday night he slipped a sleeping tablet into her tea: she enjoyed tea before going to bed. She was still asleep when they woke next morning, and to keep his son's mind off the girl, David did what Mannering had done with Bristow: sat down and checked everything. He now knew exactly where to get the high explosive, which was the last item on the list. As they discussed the project, Jonathan's excitement grew; he was ready now, and in a week's time he might be stale or too tense.

If that damned girl upstairs had been an ordinary pick-up they could have had fun and games all the week! What a bloody thing to go wrong!

He was commiserating with himself when he saw David's jaw tighten, as if he had been taken by a new and unpleasant idea, and he asked, 'What's bitten you?'

'Son,' said David softly, 'we mustn't use the car any more. We had it there when we first cased the joint. *You* had it when you picked the girl up, and we took it there to have another look. I've been trying to see if we had any blind spot, and that car's certainly one. We're going to keep it in the garage, and we'd better hire one for the rest of the week. We need some kind of transport, this week especially.'

'I can hire a jalopy, that's no problem,' Jonathan declared. 'One telephone call and I can fix it. If you're sure we have to.'

'I'm sure,' David said.

'Okay, I'll fix it,' promised his son. But he didn't move from the table, he just looked levelly at the older man, puzzling him for a few moments, until he said, 'Dad, you think I'm a fool, don't you?'

'I think you lack a lot of experience,' his father replied evasively.

'In some things, you think I'm a fool. You think I don't know we're going to have to kill Dee. You think I believe you when you say we just have to keep her quiet until the job's done. We've got to keep her quiet for always, haven't we?'

It was a long time before David Cleff recovered from his shocked surprise, and decided how to answer his son.

Finally, he said, 'Yes, Jonathan.'

Even then he did not know how the other would react.

18

Method

Neither father nor son spoke for a long time after that simple, 'Yes, Jonathan'. Jonathan looked away and then up towards a corner of the ceiling towards Deirdre's room. He pushed his chair back slowly, moved to the window and looked out on to the rainswept front garden and the street. A privet hedge seemed to be raining itself and there were pools on the grass which David had cut only yesterday.

Suddenly, Jonathan said, 'There's something about her.'

'I know,' his father replied, gently.

'I've never met a girl like her.'

'I know, Jon.'

'I think I'm in love with her.'

David did not answer.

'I'll tell you why I think so,' went on Jonathan, still staring out of the window. 'When I thought she was a spy I could have broken her neck, I — it hurt so much. I hated being tricked by her, I thought she was okay.' He paused but his father judged it not the moment to comment, and soon he went on, 'And then when you talked to her I knew it was hopeless. I'm not a fool, Dad, I really knew from the beginning it was hopeless. All I could think of was the past couple of weeks. It — it's been as if we were married.'

His father said again, 'I know, son.'

'And then I thought, we'll go on like that. I'd promise her she'd be okay when we'd done the job, so we could carry on making love — you know. I thought, I can keep her quiet, there's no need to give her this dope, I can stay with her, we can have a hell of a good time.'

In a husky voice, David said, 'Is that what you thought, Jon?'

'Yep! That's what I thought. Only — only I can't do it, Dad. I can't do it. I'd feel as if I were cheating her all the time. She's not just a tart, she — she's something special.'

'Very special,' his father agreed.

'So I know what we have to do,' stated Jonathan Cleff.

Very slowly, almost as if both thought and words hurt him, the other said,

'What do we have to do, son?'

'We have to keep her under with drugs, see. All the time. I couldn't stand it if she was dead. I couldn't stand it I tell you. So we have to keep her under with drugs.'

'We will,' promised David.

'Have you got plenty?' demanded Jonathan.

'I've plenty.'

'Where the hell do you get these things from, like the explosive and drugs?'

'I've got friends,' answered David.

'There's a lot you don't tell me, isn't there?'

'Some things I keep to myself,' David agreed.

His son looked at him broodingly for some time, and then shrugged. 'I dare say you're right. But for some things you need me.'

'I need you very much,' the older man declared.

'And it's okay?'

'Keeping Dee under, you mean?'

'Yes.'

'It's okay,' said David.

'It's the only way,' said his son. 'If she's under with the

drugs it's as if she's asleep, see? She doesn't know anything so she isn't scared and she can't look at me as if I'm lower than the animals, can she? And she won't suffer. So I can go out and have myself a good time. I can look up some of my old girl friends and throw some money about, they'll do anything for me if I'm in the money! And we can play some golf and watch Chelsea, they've got a mid-week match on Wednesday. We can just pretend she isn't up there, can't we?'

'It's the best way to handle the situation,' David assured him as if with utmost conviction. 'The kind way.'

'That's okay, then,' said Jonathan, with great relief, but he didn't turn away from his father, instead he put his hands on the square shoulders and gripped with fingers which had become very much more powerful in the past few weeks. 'But I want to see her every night. Don't give her an overdose, yet. Understand, Dad?'

'I understand,' David assured his son very quietly.

* * *

Each morning, Jonathan went to see Deirdre.

And each night.

When she did come round, during the day, she was too numb to be afraid, and David fed her a little milk and a meat extract, enough to keep her alive and to keep faith with his son.

* * *

Each morning and each evening, Anthea Ross prayed that she would get news of the car which Mannering wanted to find, but there was no message.

Each day, for as much of the time as they could spare, and for part of every evening, Mannering and Bristow opened the steel cases which contained the Jimmu Tenno treasures and placed each treasure, as with reverence, on the strong-room shelves and in the alcoves of the two rooms. To Mannering, and in a lesser degree, to Bristow, it was as if they were handling sacred relics. Most of the *objets* were small, the majority being jewelled figures of the gods of the earth, of wood and stream and valley and mountain, the work of long dead craftsmen whose faith as well as love was in all they did.

Never had Mannering seen more beautifully jewelled craftsmanship.

Some were of semi-precious stones but inlaid in such a way that they had their own almost incalculable values. Some were of precious stones of superlative quality. There were swords and rings, there were head-dresses and breast-plates, all just miniatures and none lifesize; all for the temples of the God who had, many Japanese believed, become a human being sent to rule over the nation.

Each day, Hishinoto telephoned Mannering and each day received the same answer,

'The overall value is greater than it was yesterday. I don't believe there is anything more beautiful in the world.'

On the second day, Mannering telephoned Jack Diamond, and said, 'I don't think the two million extra cover for the Jimmu Tenno treasure is anything like enough: I think it should be twice that figure, or even three times.'

'Then I shall have to cover it with the Lloyds under-writers,' Diamond replied. 'And if it's going on too long we'll need a detailed specification.'

'I would expect to be through within two weeks,' Mannering told him.

'With someone on the premises all the time, presumably.'

'Yes. Bill Bristow or me,' answered Mannering. 'In fact I expect to be here most of the week-end. My wife is fascinated by what I've told her of the treasures and she'll be here on Saturday afternoon, anyhow.'

'I won't insist that your wife stays there, provided somebody does!' retorted Diamond. 'Incidentally...'

'Yes?'

'I wouldn't mind a look at them myself!'

'Wait until Monday,' Mannering said. 'Everything will be out of its packing and on display by then.'

'Then Monday it is,' agreed Diamond. 'Oh, and another incidentally...'

'Yes?'

'You can take the Felisa Emeralds off your schedule.'

'I can? That means that Mrs. Culbertson has taken out a separate cover, presumably.'

'Quite right,' said Diamond. 'She is one of the most insurance-conscious people I know, she never leaves anything uncovered for five minutes.' He chuckled. 'And you'll be amused to know she's covering them for fifty thousand pounds, she doesn't mean to be under-insured.'

Mannering was laughing as he rang off.

When he got to Green Street that evening, he saw a green M.G. vanishing round the far corner, and wasn't surprised when he got upstairs to hear that Anthea Ross had been to see Lorna. Lorna poured him a drink before she took up her favourite position on the pouffe, and sipped a dry sherry.

'She didn't want anything in particular,' she told Mannering, 'except, I think, reassurance. It's strange that both she and Ballantine know so many people and yet seem to have so few friends.'

'They're cast in the role of advisers,' Mannering mused. 'When it comes to wanting advice themselves they don't know who to turn to. The marvel is that they acknowledge their need of it. What did Anthea have to say?'

'Should she break the engagement or not?'

'And what did you advise?'

'I didn't exactly advise,' Lorna admitted, rather forlornly. 'It is *such* a personal issue. She thinks that if she breaks the engagement and the news reaches the newspapers, Deirdre will see it and come home. I suppose what she isn't really sure about is whether Lucas needs her or Deirdre most. Apparently he seems in no doubt, but—well, Anthea finds herself wondering whether he is simply behaving honourably when he says that if he has to choose, it will be her and not Deirdre. In a funny way it's the most tragic human problem I've ever come across.'

'Tragic?' Mannering raised his eyebrows. 'I'd agree if you said the saddest, but . . .' he broke off, finished his drink, and went on moodily, 'Well I haven't been much good as a private detective in this, anyhow. I'd give almost anything to find that girl and talk to her.'

'Do you mean, give her a talking to?' asked Lorna wryly.

'No, my sweet, I mean *talk* to her. The Four-in-One place had at least one coloured member to two whites. I've checked as far as I can, and Deirdre hasn't any history of animosity towards people of colour. When Anthea said she was shocked by that outburst about a black bitch, Anthea had good reason. It was completely out of character. So, I want to try to find out why she's taken this attitude.' After a pause he went on, 'If I could think of a way to get her to come and see me I'd jump at it, but after our two encounters she probably lumps me with her father.'

'I suppose . . .' began Lorna, but didn't finish.

'What do you suppose?'

'She is all right,' Lorna said.

'In the sense that she hasn't had an accident?'

'Yes, that, and—oh, I suppose I'm being morbid!' Lorna jumped up. 'I must go and turn those steaks!' She hurried into the kitchen and they didn't discuss the problem of Deirdre and Anthea again that evening.

Over dinner, Mannering asked, 'Are you free on Saturday afternoon?'

'Yes, darling!'

'That's good,' said Mannering with obvious pleasure. 'Bill will be at the strong-room and with the three of us working without interruption all the afternoon we should get a great deal done. By the middle of next week I should be able to start the itemised valuations.'

'Are they as lovely as you first thought?'

Mannering put down his knife and fork, looked across at her, and said in the most positive of voices,

'I am inclined to think that they comprise the most beautiful and conceivably the most valuable single collection of jewellery and *objets d'art* I have ever seen outside of a museum; and even when one thinks of a museum's treasures one seldom sees such a comprehensive collection from one place. The Vatican has the most remarkable single collection, I would say, but no single group can compare with this — not even the Tutankhamun treasures. It is incomparable; and it is priceless. I am nearly sure I am going to make myself unpopular with Hishinoto,' he finished with a grimace.

'Valuing them too high?' Lorna asked.

'No. I don't think these should be split up among national museums. I think they belong to Japan and should stay there, or at most be sent overseas on loan. But before I can really make up my mind I think I am going to need a little more sustenance in the form of that steak!'

* * *

For the next three days Mannering worked harder at Quinns than he had for a long time, and by the Friday evening all but one of the cases of the Jimmu Tenno treasure was unpacked and displayed in the two inner chambers of the strong-room. Every piece added to his conviction that this was the most beautiful and valuable individual collection he had ever seen.

Handling piece after piece, comparing it with others and with illustrations of other Japanese treasures, made it possible almost to forget that the other two chambers and the safes in them were crammed with treasures in their way as priceless and as unique.

* * *

On the Friday night, Jonathan stood in the tiny room and looked down at Deirdre. She was breathing quite evenly, and even had a little colour on her cheeks; it was as if she were in a natural sleep, not under drugs. When he went downstairs he said to his father,

'I'm not going out tonight.'

'Very sensible,' his father said. 'I am going to deal with those nightwatchmen, but I want to be by myself for that. When I'm back we'll go over everything again in detail.'

He knew exactly where the two watchmen met when they finished their first rounds of Hart House, and was ready for them. He used tear-gas to overpower them, then gave them shots of morphia and bound them hand and foot. He doubted whether they would survive; but as the girl had to be killed, that was not important; only escape mattered.

'We will take only the easy-to-handle contents of the strong-room and load them into the van,' he told Jonathan when he was back. 'We shall drive the truck to Cater's Yard, paint out the name, and bring it here. We'll prise all but the named jewels out of their settings and later put them into small boxes which we already have ready and labelled. The larger pieces and the named jewellery we shall take to Putney, and transfer them to the buyer, in another van.'

'When do we collect the dough?' demanded Jonathan.

'It will be deposited in several banks in different parts of the world,' David Cleff said. 'If it isn't, I simply tip the

Yard about the buyer — but don't worry, the money will be there, at least half a million pounds for each of us.'

'Wonderful,' breathed Jonathan. 'Wonderful!'

'That's the only word,' agreed his father, fighting down his own excitement. 'But remember before we leave we have to put Dee asleep for good.'

'I know,' Jonathan said stiffly. 'I don't need reminding.'

'And remember, if anyone tries to get in our way, we kill them,' went on David.

That was the moment when, for the first time, Jonathan saw his father draw a gun from his pocket: a flat, snub-nosed automatic pistol.

19

The Drill

MANNERING TURNED INTO Hart Row just after ten o'clock that Saturday morning, later than he had intended because his car was being serviced and rather than take Lorna's, he had come by bus. Lorna would be here in her car about half-past two. He went to the end of Hart Row. Once there had been a walk through here, past the back entrance to Quinns and beyond towards Piccadilly; now there was a thick reinforced concrete wall just beyond Quinns. The dark oak beams and the centuries-old tiles looked strange against the stark concrete. But the doorway was the same, the door made of three wide planks of hand-planed oak was exactly as it had been throughout those same centuries.

As Mannering went to pull the old fashioned pull-type bell, of wrought-iron, it opened and Bristow appeared.

'Good morning, John.'

'Good morning, Bill. Waiting for me?'

'I'd been writing a few letters,' Bristow said, 'and saw you out of the window.' They went inside. 'There's nothing much in the post — certainly nothing that won't keep until Monday.'

'Then we'll go straight into the strong-room,' Mannering decided.

Soon they were in the third chamber, one removed from

the new concrete wall; one removed, then, from the ramp of the big new office block which gave it illusory protection.

* * *

Jonathan Cleff was sweating as he turned off New Bond Street and into Hart Row. Two elderly women were in the street but neither looked up. Quinns window was empty and the security lights showed at the back of the shop. The truck moved into the courtyard; a Vauxhall Cresta and a big black Rover were the only other vehicles parked.

'Mannering's not here!' exclaimed Jonathan.

'He put his stint in last week-end,' his father said with airy assurance. It was no use telling Jonathan again that if Mannering or anyone else was at Quinns and threatened discovery, he would kill.

Jonathan drove to the position he had taken up the previous Saturday, and then reversed so that he could drive straight away; and this way, with the tail-board down, the truck could be more easily loaded. Covered by old cement sacks and canvas were dozens of small, light-weight cases, no larger than attaché cases.

Both men jumped down, and dragged a sign from the truck and placed it in the gap between the front of the truck and the wall. It said in bold letters: ROAD UP. They dropped some of the sacks, a bag of cement and some bricks near the sign and then hauled a small hand-operated concrete mixer down. With this in position so that anyone who chanced to see the truck would also see the evidence of work, they eased the drill down from the truck.

In the wall of the garage was an electric point or outlet, and the drill plug was made for this. 'No one will take any notice, even if they pass us,' David said, to keep Jonathan's nerve steady.

Jonathan pushed the plug in and then placed the pile-driver of the drill lightly on the concrete near to the spot where they were nearest the wall of Quinns. He held the drill firmly in both hands, and then looked up at his father, who smiled faintly and nodded.

'Up to you now, son,' he said laconically.

The drill began to roar and jump and quiver, but it did not move from the spot where Jonathan had placed it. Slowly it began to bite into the concrete until at last cracks appeared in several directions. Jonathan lifted the drill and placed it carefully on one of the cracks, where more cracks appeared at once. He glanced up in triumph at his father, who nodded. Soon, a pile of chippings, both large and small appeared, and David used a spade to scrape them away some distance from the cracks.

In the confined space of the ramp the roar of the drill was very loud, but it hardly stopped. Every now and again Jonathan looked up with a grin, as if to say, 'Look how good I am,' and each time David gave him a nod of congratulation. David kept clearing the chippings away and used a pickaxe to pry up some heavy pieces, then a wheelbarrow to wheel them further into the courtyard.

Suddenly, the drill struck the steel wire which reinforced the wall. David used a pair of electric wire cutters which went through the steel without difficulty. They rested for a few moments and then went on again.

David said, 'It's shown as five feet thick. You've got through three already.'

'Just give me time,' breathed Jonathan.

* * *

'I think we should have a rest,' Mannering said. 'I'm getting hungry, too.'

'I've some ham and cheese upstairs,' Bristow told him.

Up the narrow and twisting old stairs they went and into a tiny room which led off a tiny kitchen. When

Bristow opened the window the sound of a pneumatic drill came clearly.

'I wonder where that is,' Mannering said idly.

'Piccadilly, probably,' replied Bristow. 'Sounds travel in the oddest way up here,' He took a damp cloth off a pile of substantial and appetising sandwiches, then made some instant coffee. Inside half an hour each of them was ready to go back to work. Bristow closed the window but the sound of the drilling continued. They did not hear it in the shop or in Mannering's office but when they were in the strong-room it was just audible.

'More repairs in Hart House,' Bristow remarked. 'We shall come here one day and find Quinns buried under a pile of concrete!' They worked steadily for another forty minutes before Mannering went upstairs to see if Lorna had arrived. He walked towards the courtyard of the office block and saw her coming from her car, a Morris 1100. Over by the entrance to the ramp was a builder's truck, a road work sign and the noise of a pneumatic drill. A man who was covered in white dust was shovelling gravel into a small concrete mixer.

Lorna dusted her shoulders as they reached Hart Row, but neither made any comment. They stepped inside and closed and locked the door, then went downstairs. The sound of the drill was more distant but quite unmistakable down there. Bristow was standing back and studying a set of temple dancers, exquisite models which made Lorna exclaim aloud.

Gradually she took in the treasures about her.

Mannering had never had a moment's doubt about the significance of the Jimmu Tenno treasure, but now he saw the effect on a woman who loved beautiful things but, where *objets d'art* were concerned, was not an expert. She picked up one model as if she were frightened she would hurt it, then turned from one to another, absolutely entranced.

The distant rumble of the pneumatic drill went on and on.

Mannering was aware of it and yet not remotely alarmed; he was transfixed by Lorna's expression, by the radiance in her eyes. She put first one *objet* down and then another looking at each as if she could not believe her eyes.

The rumble stopped.

'John,' Lorna breathed, 'how beautiful. How unbelievably beautiful.'

'Yes,' Mannering said. 'I have never seen anything lovelier.'

He broke off . . .

He was looking towards the archway which led to the next and last chamber where the larger pieces were and where the lights were on, and a movement caught his eye. He thought, stupidly, that it could not be a movement, it must be an illusion. Then it came again, a shadow moving. Bristow and Lorna were looking at the jewels and for a split second he could hardly draw breath.

The shadow moved again.

It was an arm, outstretched; and there was the shape of a hand and of a gun.

He knew on that very instant what the drilling had been; he knew why it had stopped. The wall had been breached but the light from the garage ramp was poor, this shadow was cast by the neon lighting inside the vaults. He was sure that at least one armed man was in the other chamber, close to the entrance to this one. He knew where the man must be standing, and that Lorna and then Bristow would be first in the line of fire.

Bristow, puzzled by his sudden silence, looked towards him.

Mannering put a finger to his lips, and said,

'Priests and princes used to worship these.'

Lorna, still entranced, said huskily, 'I don't wonder.'

'Bill,' Mannering said, fighting to make himself sound normal. 'I left my keys in my desk.'

Bristow, staring now towards the shadow, asked in a hoarse voice, 'What keys, John?'

'The safe keys. They're in my midde drawer. Will you go and get them?'

There were no keys in the middle drawer but there was a key in Mannering's hand as he held it out to Bristow. Bristow moistened his lips, and then gulped. *There were no keys in the drawer but Mannering kept a revolver there.*

'Until I have them I can't open the safe,' Mannering said, testily.

'I'll go and get them,' Bristow offered. It looked as if it took a tremendous physical effort for him to force himself to move away from the opening to the next chamber, take the key and pass Mannering. It would be thirty seconds at least, perhaps a full minute before he reached the office and got back, and his movements were slow and stiff, as if he had been struck with sudden paralysis. But he took the key and he did pass, and his pace quickened.

'Lorna, love,' Mannering called.

She didn't look round, but said, 'John, I can't believe it.'

'You wait until I get that safe open,' Mannering said, with great enthusiasm. 'Come and look at this one — it's the smallest of them all.'

She turned slowly, reluctant to look away from the treasures.

There was no safe near Mannering, and she looked puzzled.

'Look at what?' she asked.

'This, stupid,' he said as if half-vexed, and beckoned her. Startled, she moved towards him. She wore a golden brown suit, loose-fitting and perfect for her. She had never seemed more beautiful — nor more scared as she realised something was amiss.

If the man or men in the other chamber appeared now, and used the gun, the bullet could not miss her. She faltered. He stretched out his empty hand and with the false realism in his voice made himself say, 'Don't drop it!' But his hand *was* empty.

He took hers.

On the instant he stepped in front of her and at the same time thumbed a movement towards the other opening. She could not fail to understand what he meant, that she was to go into the other chamber where Bristow must have gone, but she still hesitated, as if reluctant to leave him here alone. This didn't matter so much now, he was between her and anyone in that fourth chamber. He stood quite still.

The shadow moved again and there was no doubt at all about the shape of the gun.

How long had Bristow been gone? Thirty seconds? Forty? The full minute? Mannering felt icy cold, now. He glanced round. Lorna had done what he had told her to, he was alone in this chamber. He moved to the cover of one wall, pitched his voice low as if he were speaking from the other side of the chamber, and said,

'It's a perfect miniature.'

Lorna should have answered, to make that sound convincing.

He spread himself against the wall. If the man holding the gun came through the opening then he would not see Mannering at first; he would see the chamber empty of people in spite of the scintillating brilliance of the tiny models and the treasures there.

From the fourth chamber there came a whisper, '*Can you see anyone?*'

A word came from someone else, and sounded like, '*Quiet.*'

Then he saw the gun; the hand of the man holding it. He heard the first man gasp,

'It's empty!'

He saw the other leap forward, gun in hand, and swivelled round towards him. He saw a middle-aged man coated with dust, his eyes unnaturally bright in his pale face look towards him and raise the gun to shoot. He, John Mannering, was only a second away from death.

He heard the roar of a shot from the second chamber, and saw this man stagger and fall. Out of the corner of his eyes he saw Bristow. He heard a cry of alarm from the fourth chamber and a cry which sounded like, '*Dad. My God! Dad!*' The man who had been shot was sprawling on the floor. Another man was standing above him, covered in the white dust.

In the calmest of voices Bristow called, 'Stay where you are!'

Instead of making the second man stand still, the order galvanised him into action. He turned and ran; and as he ran, the man on the floor made a convulsive movement and then obviously tried to throw something at Mannering and Bristow. But it went the other way. Mannering realised on the instant what it was and shouted, 'Down, Bill, down!' and flung himself on his face.

But he was in no danger. Nor was Bristow or Lorna, although she appeared in the doorway of the third chamber. For David Cleff had tossed the container of high explosive, the 'better than nitro-glycerine' in the wake of his son, who took the full force of the explosion.

When Mannering reached him the top of his head had disappeared.

* * *

'They're both dead,' Mannering told Lorna, gently.

'John, who — who were they?'

'I don't know. They don't appear to have had any identification on them,' Mannering answered. 'They'll be identified before long, of course. Darling, I'll have to stay a while to help clear up the mess in the fourth chamber and search for any of the jewels which might have been damaged. I wish you'd go home.'

'I'm as capable of staying here as you are,' Lorna retorted firmly. 'The bodies have been taken away haven't they?'

'Yes,' Mannering answered. 'And the police are searching the truck outside. These two came prepared for a big haul, there's no doubt about that.' He looked up as Bristow, who had been with the police, came into the office. 'Hallo, Bill. Is there anything fresh?'

'No,' Bristow answered, 'nothing at all. There are a lot of questions to be answered, John. No one would have attempted this without an assured market for a lot of the goods, and until we know the would-be buyer I'll be an unhappy man.'

'I'll bet you will,' Mannering said. 'And but for you I'd be a dead man. We'd better get downstairs again. Lorna's going to help.'

As they worked among the debris, their spirits rose. None of the Jimmu Tenno treasures appeared to have been damaged, for those in the fourth chamber had been out of the mainstream of the blast, much of which had been drawn through the hole drilled into the cellar wall.

* * *

All this time, Deirdre lay unconscious in the house at Wimbledon.

20

The Man who Remembered

ONLY A FEW yards away from Deirdre the red Mini stood in the wooden garage, and across the road from the Cleff house an elderly Jamaican gardener looked at the closed doors. He was alone; he spent most of his time alone and at work, meeting with others only at church on Sundays and at church social meetings during the week. He worked for a young couple who did not harass him because he was slow or because he came in at odd hours, since his back hurt so much that sometimes he could hardly bend to touch the soil he loved.

His name was Benedict Samms.

Because he was alone so much and had been trained to read in his native Jamaican Kingston, he read a great deal including the newspaper and the journal which brought him news of home. That Saturday as he sat in the toolshed of the house opposite the Cleffs, he took out a folded, mimeographed sheet of local news about his own local community and spread this on his knee as he opened a packet of sandwiches which he had brought with him for lunch. The lady of the house would bring him some tea a little later.

He read the little sheet line by line.

He read the short paragraph which said that if anyone had seen a small red car, a Morris Mini with the number

YXL 1243, they were asked to telephone Mrs. Anthea Ross, at a Kensington telephone number. Anthea Ross had a great reputation among him and his friends and acquaintances; if anyone could help her they would do so eagerly.

He looked across at the closed doors, and said to himself, 'That surely was a red Mini, yes, sir. It surely was.'

And a few minutes afterwards he added in the same deep monotone, 'It sure had a number like 1234, it surely did.'

He was still pondering this, not so much excited as curious, when the tall young husband came in carrying a huge breakfast cup of tea and some chocolate biscuits. These two met only on Saturdays, and as Benedict seldom came on Saturday afternoons this was a rare meeting.

'Don't get up, Ben,' the young man said. He looked like a freckled boy as he placed cup and plate on a box and then sat on the edge of a small workbench and chatted for a few minutes about the state of the country; in fact he was fascinated by the old man's deep voice and his slow utterance.

'Mr. Hill, sah, I wonder if you could help me on a small matter,' asked Benedict, and the red-haired youth replied 'Yes' immediately, for this man had never asked for help before. 'I just wondered, sir, do you happen to remember the number of the motor car the people across the road have?' He held up the journal, pointing out the paragraph, and added, 'That Mrs. Ross, she surely is a great lady, sir, if I could be of assistance to her I would be very glad to.'

Hill glanced at the car number and then across the road, and at last he said, 'Do you know, Ben, I think it *is* YXL 1243. But there's a boy next door who knows every car number in the street. I'll go and ask him in a minute.' He glanced through the paper and went on, 'Why would this Mrs. Ross want the number, do you know?'

'No, sir, I don't know a thing more than it says there,'

Benedict Samms told him. 'But I do know it would be for a good reason or Mrs. Ross wouldn't want to know. You can be absolutely sure of that, sir.'

* * *

Mannering heard the telephone ringing from a long way off, and straightened up from the rubble which he was sifting. He did not think anything was missing, now. All the Jimmu Tenno treasures had been taken into the third chamber which could be sealed off from the second chamber with a steel door electronically controlled. The police were working on the other side of the garage wall, and from the fourth chamber he could see and hear them. Bristow was at another pile of the rubble, Lorna was straightening some of the *objets* in the third chamber, and called,

'I'll go!'

Mannering expected her to come back to say it was a newspaperman.

'Nothing more here,' Bristow observed. 'But we'll have it all sifted again, won't we?'

'With a fine-tooth comb,' Mannering assured him. He raised his head. 'What's that?' 'That' was Lorna calling in obvious excitement and he strode to the next chamber and met her at the foot of the stairs. Excitement blazed from her eyes as she cried, 'Anthea's on the telephone, she couldn't get us at the flat so tried here. One of her people has identified the red Mini!'

Mannering could not get to the telephone quickly enough.

'Anthea!... This is more wonderful than you think... Are you absolutely sure? If you are, I must tell the police at once.'

'John, I'm certain,' Anthea replied with complete certainty. 'I won't try to explain, but it usually stands outside the garage of a small house in Cobbold Street, Wimbledon, and it's probably in the garage now. You did say you'll tell the police, didn't you?'

'Yes, at once,' Mannering said.

'Will it help if Lucas and I come to Cobbold Street?' asked Anthea. 'It's the first glimmer of hope we've had.'

'It certainly can't do any harm,' Mannering answered. 'It may be another disappointment, though. I'll be there within an hour,' he added. 'I must rush now.'

He rang off and turned to see Bristow, who said quietly, 'If I talk to the Inspector in charge outside he'll move very fast.'

'Will you, quickly?' asked Mannering. 'And are you coming to Wimbledon?'

'One of us should stay here,' Bristow advised. 'I'll be glad to.'

He went out to see the Yard man.

Soon, the Mannerings followed him. The strong-room was sealed off at the third chamber and as safe as it had always been except at the chamber which had been so badly damaged. Police were in strength in Hart Row and in the courtyard of Hart House, and 'Absolute' Abbott was among them, while a dozen men were walking among the rubble by the truck and the concrete mixer. Mannering took the wheel of Lorna's car as Abbott cleared a path for him.

He knew that the Inspector would talk to the Yard, and the Yard would flash instructions to the Wimbledon police, so that within minutes 19 Cobbold Street would be surrounded. He could imagine that Sir Lucas Ballantine was already on the way to join Anthea, who was nearer Wimbledon. He wondered whether this could possibly lead to Deirdre, and the next moment he wondered who worked with the two thieves in this, who had been prepared to buy from them. Now and again he and Lorna exchanged a word or two, but they said very little. Both were dishevelled and dust-strewn; and both were anxious as well as inwardly excited.

As they neared Wimbledon Common, driving up Putney Hill, Lorna said, 'Even if Deirdre is found it won't solve the family problem.'

Mannering simply commented, 'No.' But nothing was likely to depress him at that moment.

* * *

The small boy who knew all the car numbers in Cobbold Street and vicinity, together with red-headed Bill and his chubby wife, old Benedict Samms and dozens of others in the street watched as a force of police surrounded Number 19, and then sent two men to break down the door of the garage. It took only minutes to open the padlock and the doors. The little red Mini stood facing them, surrounded by shelves on which tools and jars of screws and nuts and bolts stood cheek by jowl with cans of oil and tins of paint. Checking this took five minutes. Fifteen minutes after the police had first arrived, two plainclothes men went to the front door and knocked and rang, while others tried the back door. Everything was done with painstaking slowness. A message at last reached the front door from the back.

'The back door's bolted, sir.'

'Then we'll have to break this one down,' the Wimbledon Inspector decided.

Two big men put their shoulders to the door, which creaked and groaned until finally it gave way. Immediately they began a cautious search of the whole house, going from room to room. It was five minutes before they came to the locked door, and by chance it was the Inspector who turned the key, which was on the outside, and pushed the door open.

'My God!' he breathed.

And he stood absolutely still for a moment, for it was as if he were staring at a corpse. A man behind him looked over his shoulder, gulped, and said, 'Shall I get a doctor, sir?'

'Yes.'

'Right, sir.'

The inspector went forward hesitantly, then saw with relief that the woman on the bed was breathing; he checked her pulse and confirmed that she was alive. He opened one eye and was familiar enough with the effects of drugs to know from the pin-point pupils that this woman had been put under with morphine. Another man joined him but they did not attempt to move the woman until a doctor arrived, a police surgeon who lived near by.

'Get her to hospital fast,' he ordered.

The ambulance was already on its way, and when Ballantine and Anthea turned into Cobbold Street, Deirdre was being carried from the house. Ballantine's quiet, 'I think that is my daughter,' was enough to make the police allow them to pass.

She looked so pale; so near to death, if not already dead.

The police surgeon, a youngish man, said confidently, 'She will be all right, sir, care and attention is all she needs. Don't worry.'

That was when the Mannerings turned into the street.

They were with Ballantine and Anthea just long enough to hear that the news was good, and to arrange to meet in the evening. Immediately after this Ballantine followed the ambulance to the hospital while Mannering, who knew the Wimbledon Inspector slightly, went into the house. There were all the records they could hope to find; the banks where packets of jewels were to have been sent; tickets for the different flights; the false passports.

And there was a list of things to do, a plan of the whole day from the time they were to set out to the time when the truck was to be left at a builder's yard in Putney. The time for that was five o'clock.

'There's still time to get it there,' said Mannering fighting back his excitement.

The Wimbledon man called the Yard, who took seconds to arrange for the truck which had been used for the raid to be taken to the rendezvous. Bristow was in a police car which followed, and was with a group who watched from a safe distance.

Mannering and Lorna watched from the roof of a nearby school.

At fifteen minutes after five a plain van turned into the yard and parked close to the truck. The driver and his companion got out and went straight to the truck, looking about them with great care but obviously not troubled. As they lowered the tailboard, three policemen who had been covered by tarpaulin sprang out and other policemen closed in. The couple from the van did not even have a chance to run.

Suddenly Mannering gripped Lorna's arm, and said unbelievingly, 'There's a man and a woman — a woman I know. That's Edith Culbertson!'

Edith Culbertson was looking straight at Bristow and had a curious kind of dignity, which did not wilt when Mannering approached. Her companion was a youngish man, who looked utterly appalled.

'Mr. Mannering,' Edith said. 'I loved the jewels and everything you had so much and I simply wasn't prepared to pay the price. I would pay what Cleff asked for them, and I tried. I think I shall always be glad that I tried,' she added in a whispering voice.

* * *

It was a week before the damage to the strong-room was repaired.

It was a week before Mannering finished the valuation of the Jimmu Tenno treasures, and talked to Hishinoto.

'If you will take them back and keep them for Japan, I'll make no charge for the valuation,' he said. 'Just to have seen them was well worth while.'

The Japanese replied: 'I will report your recommendation and your generosity to my government, Mr. Mannering.'

It was a week, also, before Deirdre Ballantine was able to leave the nursing home where she had been recovering from the drugs and from shock. Her father had seen her each day, but Anthea had stayed away. The Mannerings had been twice, and it was John who fetched her from the nursing home.

'Deirdre,' he said, 'I want to tell you how the police came to find you.' He told her quietly of the pondering and the patience of Benedict Samms, and he told her how deeply so many people felt for Anthea Ross.

'I know,' Deirdre replied. 'I've known that since I was a child. Mr. Mannering, you once asked me why I was behaving so badly about my father and Anthea, and you weren't really convinced that it was because of her colour, were you?'

'No,' Mannering replied. 'Some might feel strongly about mixed marriages but I didn't think you would. I thought you much more likely to judge by the nature and the character of the human being, not race or colour. Was I wrong?'

'No,' Deirdre said huskily. 'Not wrong.'

'Then why do you hate her so?'

Deirdre said in a low-pitched voice, 'I didn't want him to marry anyone. I knew I would lose him. I wasn't going to marry, I was going to devote my life to him. I thought — I thought that sex was just fun and children were unimportant, that I just wanted to dedicate my life to him.

'Because,' she added, her voice breaking, 'he is a very great man.

'I knew he wouldn't marry any ordinary woman, and I knew how extraordinary Anthea is, and I knew I would lose him, I tell you.' When Mannering didn't answer she went on, 'At least you're honest. You aren't trying to pretend that I can share him. I can't, you know. They will become roving ambassadors for good race relations! I know, I know. I should want that, but in fact I hated the thought.'

'Hated?' Mannering echoed, with a quick flash of hope.

'Yes,' she said. 'Hated. I don't, now. I suppose I've been too near to death. And it isn't only that I've had time to think. If I tell you something will you swear to keep it entirely to yourself — not even tell your wife, because she might tell Anthea.'

'I shall tell no one,' Mannering promised.

'Thank you,' said Deirdre, simply. 'In a way I was in love with Jonathan Cleff. We lived together for — for a week or two. Even with him, a man I could never spend my life with, I found a different kind of happiness, a physical joy and a physical hunger. Somewhere there must be a man I want to marry. And even if there isn't,' she added with tears in her eyes, 'I know how Daddy and Anthea feel towards each other. I can't rob them of that. I simply can't.'